The Evolution of Confusion ...4 of 5 (Where From Here?)

Stephen Meiner

Published by Stephen Meiner, 2023.

This is a work of fiction. Similarities to real people, places, or events are entirely coincidental.

THE EVOLUTION OF CONFUSION ...4 OF 5 (WHERE FROM HERE?)

First edition. February 4, 2023.

ISBN: 979-8215561256

Written by Stephen Meiner.

Hi, my name is Samuel ...and I'm going to write a story about Shannon, my oldest sister, whom I think is *a most unique* sister. Others may say that the best way to describe her is that she is really cool. She certainly is that, but I like to say she's unique.

Shannon is helping with Homeschooling today. I think some of the lessons are strange, but she adds such a good perspective to it all. She makes it interesting with her comments. For instance, today's assignment says to write a story about a nightmare of the worst kind. Shannon makes a face that's rather indescribable, sort of in response to the writing about nightmares. It seems like an odd subject, unless the writing is being graded by Stephen King.

Shannon says it's best to face our fears. But, the best way is *not* through sharing horror stories to see who can come up with the most frightening one. She feels the best way to face fears is through prayer. And she believes we can thank Mom that we don't often have nightmares. That was one of Mom's prayers.

My language book gives two short nightmare examples. Here is the first one:

Penelope can't believe it! She had just been asked out by the captain of the football team. Why would anyone even notice her? And he was always flirting with the other girls, especially the cheerleaders. Though when it came to the big Homecoming dance, who did he ask? He asked plain old Penelope.

Everyone else agreed she was rather old-fashioned. That's why they called her Plain o' Penelope. But, maybe he saw the beauty behind her old ways. She could be considered pretty, she contemplates as she looks in the mirror.

A pimple!

When dating the captain of the football team, plain old can quickly digress. After all, employed to think as an average teenager, Penelope is vulnerable to the adage of beauty being only skin deep. And with typical teenage analysis, this pimple becomes a nightmare of the worst kind.

I said the story was silly. Shannon laughed like only she can laugh. She said it reminded her of a true story. She said when she was my age, she got her first pimple. And it was a humongous one!

Shannon laughs again, as she remembers more about the story. Mom often had conversations with herself ...probably not aware that she thinks aloud. It's common for Mom to reason out the possibilities before drawing her own conclusions. And then the conclusion is that it doesn't matter what the possibilities are ...children are too precious to rule out anything. On this particular occasion, Mom had convinced herself that Shannon really had a cancerous skin growth.

Yes, Mom is precious the way she often overreacts for all the right reasons. And cancer is not something to mess with. So, at ten o'clock in the evening, the five of us rush to the 24-hour clinic. Shannon said I was a baby at the time, so before the journey began, Mom quickly tied some string to all my toys before duct-taping the strings to the ceiling of the van. And with all the toys dangling before my eyes, Shannon said I was so utterly content. But, to keep us all distracted at this late hour, Mom also stopped at McDonald's to get us all French Fries.

When we got to the clinic, Shannon said that everyone had been so busy eating the fries that nobody noticed that I had pulled down all the toys, and the duct-tape with them. Shannon said it was a mystery how, but I had somehow managed to get the duct-tape across my little nose and mouth. Mom concluded that it was good that we were all just outside the clinic while finishing up our fries ...because they were able to rush me in and quickly revive me.

Shannon said Mom was so relieved after that frightening event that she found an after-midnight ice cream shop near there, and treated us all. Then upon finishing that treat, Shannon asked Mom about the cancer on her cheek ...to which Mom replied, "Don't worry; it's probably just a pimple!"

Shannon says that Mom will probably insist that we all go through a thing called courtship when we get older. But, Shannon said that she hopes when I grow up, that I'm the kind of man who learns to treat people and pimples the same special way; so girls don't think pimples should be covered with powders and creams, but with French Fries and ice cream.

Shannon has a great sense of humor, I think. But, she is more than just humorous. She can be serious too. Here is the second story she read to me:

As a police officer, everyone called him Cop Cooper, except his wife. She affectionately called him Rocky. He had a gravelly voice, but he also had a soft side that he didn't usually show.

Sandy is 43 years old. She and her husband had thought they'd never have children. But, to their surprise, Sandy gets pregnant. Shortly after that, they have to face some unwelcome news. During a police chase, Rocky had steered away from a near collision with an innocent driver, resulting in his own speeding vehicle colliding with a tree. Rocky is unconscious, in critical condition.

Rocky surprises everyone with his recovery. When the baby is born, he wheels himself to the birthing unit.

4

Now it's a week before Christmas, three years later. He considers the past three years of his life, his best. Although wheelchair-ridden, he is at least able to live his greatest accomplishment, their daughter, Crystal.

They are at the clothing store where Mom wants to buy their precious little Crystal some new shoes. Rocky remarks, "A child's feet are like corn on a hot August night. Last night I could hear her feet grow. Must've just popped right out of her shoes."

Rocky isn't really into the shoe experience. He figures if the shoe fits, wear it …yet, he smiles as he hears Mom chime in, "Oh, do you like this pair, Crystal?"

Rocky looks at his own shoes. They'll never wear out. He will never walk again. Then that old feeling returns …actually, not that old, but since his terrible accident. It had taken a while to come to grips with having been a cop, a servant of the people, then suddenly feeling he was a burden to society. The fact that he is out in public doesn't help any. He can be the 'best Dad in the world', but what is he contributing to society?

His wife's voice is now distant as she continues her rapture, "Oh my, I didn't even see this rack! They're on sale!"

Suddenly, Rocky is in his old world. A teenage boy is shoplifting a pair of those air-cushioned tennis shoes, the 'way overpriced' ones. Rocky isn't totally helpless. He can quickly wheel to the corner and cut him off.

He is about to nab the boy, when too late he realizes it is a setup. The teen drops the shoes he'd concealed under his jacket, and runs in one direction as an older and bigger teen runs out the door with Crystal.

Rocky's horrified look meets his wife's, desperately pleading for that reality to be not true, while truly thinking, "I thought she was with you!" Then Rocky quickly calls for, and depends on other cops to take over …placing Crystal's life in their hands.

Often when we are caught in a situation we don't want to be in, we blame others. Yet, this is not the case with Rocky and Sandy. They both had reacted the way the teens had wanted them to. They had planned a day together, and were enjoying it ...who would blame them, saying they shouldn't have let their guard down? Why would anyone even want to leave the house if having to constantly keep their guard up?

Can anyone really say it was their fault? Well, they could say it, but they would be wrong. Nonetheless, it sends them headlong into an inconsolable nightmare of the worst kind ...that will live on and on, as a torturous memory.

I think Shannon knew I'd prefer this story over the other one because I find law enforcement people interesting. I often wonder how they think. Dad was not a police officer like Rocky, but he worked in a prison. I think a lot about what things he would've possibly thought about on the job on a daily basis. Since Dad disappeared before I was born, I was never able to get a true sense of Dad, but that never prevented me from imagining based on things I do know. Time and time again, I've seen the videos. And Dad seemed totally committed to family.

Now, when I read the articles about the prison break, they make it seem like Dad helped the prisoner escape, and that would also make it seem like he skipped out on his family. Facts are not always facts, yet they are presented anyway.

If facts are presented in the courtroom, there are usually many opposing facts presented. Yet, it isn't just in a court case that these dramas play out. In everyday life, people don't always want to know the truth.

I would think that people would want to know the absolute truth, if they could know it ...but, sadly people often prefer their own way, instead of the true way. Regardless, there is only one absolute truth.

Wishful thinking doesn't bring about truth. Denial doesn't change what actually is true. Accepting blindly doesn't help. Nor does doubting one's character, without reason. All these common ways of thinking can only sell one guarantee ...that they all aid in clouding judgment, and distorting the truth.

But, trust is a crucial aspect of our life, and we have to start somewhere. This seems so very complex, but not so complex if one begins with what really matters ...looking to the true character. And just like lies almost always require more lies, and more sophisticated ones; truth also builds truth. And it will be solid, as long as the foundation isn't destroyed.

* * * * * * *

My assignment was to write about a nightmare, but Shannon says she thinks that is not necessary. She said it was enough of a nightmare having to deal with what happened to Dad, but she said I don't need to focus on the 'bad'. There are stories to be told, and each of us kids have our own part in the story which began with Dad & Mom ...though Shannon will add, "I know you know the story actually begins with God."

My story?? It isn't really so complex ...I'm just making it confusing. I'm not trying to make it that way. I realize that complexity often breeds disinterest. So, I want to keep it simple, but to be honest with you, my life has not been that simple. I guess my life hasn't been that much more difficult than anyone else's in my family, and I apologize if I seem to come across as saying my life is as difficult as that of some of you readers. Yet, I'm sure that those of you without dads can relate somewhat.

In my family, I'm the youngest. My sisters and brother have some real memories of being with Dad. I only have the videos. I don't know who has it the worst—-they loved him so much, and now miss him so much—-and I never had the chance to know him in real life as they did. I have difficulty relating to all this. And I guess that's why I relate better with my older sister. I admire her free and adventurous spirit. Imagining things like Arabian horses running down sandy beaches, now that's her dream. She doesn't bog herself down with other drama.

Life's experiences bring both the good and the bad your way. When faced with the more difficult things in life, we just have to learn to cope. If the bad never happens, then great! Live as happy as you can.

And yes, it's good to be informed about things. Ignorance is not always bliss. Mom has always been good with setting us straight on things. We shouldn't just dream dreams ...we have to live our lives. And when you begin your own family, there should be new parameters. And time is one of the most valuable quantities. Mom said that was one of the biggest struggles for her.

Dad had begun to write a book, entitled *The Essence,* two years before he and Mom got married. He had time back then. I've heard a few relatives say they felt Dad took responsibility too seriously. Though whether it was a sense of family responsibility, or his doubts whether what he began writing was important enough to invest more time in ...whatever the reason, Dad stopped writing.

The phone is ringing. Sorry, I'll get back with you!

Okay, I'm back. You won't believe this! My cousin just called. She has a wonderful adventure she is going on. And she wants my sister to go on it with her. I wish I could go too, but I'm too young.

I'm sure Mom will try to talk my sister out of it. Mom is very protective of us. She always says that being an adult doesn't mean you don't have to listen to her; you just get to make your final decision after listening to what she has to say. I'm not at that adult stage, but Shannon is. I've got a feeling this is going to happen for Shannon, yet it's always hard to go against Mom's advice.

Anyway, this is just a little about me ...enough to give me credit for a short story. You probably don't want to hear much of what I'd say anyway. And if you were somehow mildly interested, I'd probably only lose you somewhere along the way ...so, I'm going to stop before that happens.

I couldn't begin the story because I wasn't born yet. So, you will just have to start without me. Yet, if you read fast enough, you can catch up with the rest of us on this adventure stuff.

Dad was a very interesting person, it seems. But, one thing for sure ...he kept poor notes. That is something we seem all to agree with.

Mom is trying to figure it all out. For some reason, she feels now is the time she is meant to attempt to write it.

* * * * * * *

Don't read too fast, or you'll get ahead of her.

XXVII.

When Shannon had first found Dad's writing. She had felt it was a 'first draft', but it looks like it had been drafted and went to war ...and lost. And there were also confusing thoughts written down explaining his ambivalence over whether he should pursue on with his original idea of *'The Essence'*.

Cindy found it all so confusing, as if some sort of legible sense could be made from all the barrage of thoughts ...as if something meaningful could evolve out of the mess, and emerge from the page. She felt it was quite appropriate to be entitled, *'The Evolution of Confusion'*.

Shannon had offered to help her with it, but Cindy felt it was unfair to expect someone so young and full of energy to be bogged down with such an undertaking. Shannon has a promising life ahead of her ...a life she should have every opportunity to live.

Shannon had fairly much forgotten about Stan. But Fernye hadn't. In his late twenties, and still single. Fernye prays about her secret wish. And if her prayers are to be answered in the way she wants them to be, Stan will not be single much longer.

Fernye understands that prayers are not always answered in the way we would desire them to be. The Bible says that God's thoughts are not our thoughts. And Fernye has long since reconciled her thoughts on that. God loves us, and He knows better than us what is best for us. But as she sees it, God will not fault her for having her secret wishes ...and as wishful and far removed as they may seem to be, it is possible that God will grant her the desires of her heart.

George and Stan were spending much time overseas. Presently, they were residing in Jerusalem. Fernye had a secret in reference to that also. She had been keeping in touch with Stan. George was there on diplomatic relations ....and Stan was always there by his side, learning much. Though the peace process was making some headway, it always seemed to fall short of the grand expectations. This is where Fernye's secret came into play. She had outlined precisely what she felt Stan should do.

Stan had been silent up until now. But this was his advantage. When he finally did speak, it took both George and the others in the meeting by surprise.

Stan stands up, "I do not understand how you are to arrive at peace through demands, compromise, and concessions. It is not fair to ask someone to give up something, especially with no clear understanding of how important it is to them. Therefore, I would like to spend one week with each of the representative groups here: to tour each and every one of your countries, enter your homes and holy places, and to experience your visions."

And that's exactly what happens. Stan and George are treated as honored guests. And as they walk about the land, there is total peace for that first week, the second week, and on through to the prearranged seventh week—-after each representative group had taken their turn in playing host to this living experience.

The seventh week they meet again. This meeting has a very different tone to it. It is similar to the first meeting by the fact that it is all men, but this time ...the men do not appear so harsh.

Stan has a broad smile as he addresses his newly acquainted friends, "For the first seven days after we last met, there was peace. Into the second week and through the third, there was peace. As we went forth through the fourth, and challenged the doubts of so many by completing the fifth, it seemed inversely improbable that we would not find peace for a sixth and seventh week. Now today, I ask each of you, 'How long will the peace last?'"

Stan continues to capture their interest, "When the peace lasted seven days, few believed it could last a second week. Now that it has lasted seven weeks, I ask you, how much longer do you believe it can last? But before you answer that, let me share with you something I've experienced with each and every one of you through those seven weeks. I did not experience a difference of people. What I felt was a common bond, not any difference significant enough to have fought for, the centuries over. Truly, there has been fighting and hatred—-but not over what any of you truly represent. You've been fighting over a misplaced emotion. You've been fighting over a hurt in the past. You continue to hurt each other in the most horrific ways, over a misunderstanding of the past. And unless it stops, and you've shown that you can stop it, your children and your children's children will be fighting over what you are fighting over today. They will not understand it, but they will fight because you have fought. You will not pass on to them a blessing, as fathers should pass on to their children, but you will pass on to them your pain. You will pass on to them the fight."

Stan looks about. They are listening to him. Over the course of the past weeks, he's endeared himself to them. "And when they die—-when your children die—-your wives will cry and perhaps you will cry, if you have any tears left in you. But most likely you will continue to do what you've been doing—-you will go out and kill again. But let me make one thing clear. When you kill—-be not mistaken, the children will not die because of some stranger you presently call your enemy. The children will die because of you. You are killing your own children because you choose to pass on the fight. It's because of *you*! If we filled this room here with just your preschool children, they'd get along. But if we allowed *you* to visit them, they would perish at each others' hands—-all because of *your* hatred."

Stan leans forward, whispering loudly, "I beg of you, go home and love your children. And if one person kills another, don't hate those people. Teach your children to hate the hatred. Admit your mistakes and join together in communion and heal the land. I've communed with each of you. I've felt each of your hurts, but I cannot feel your hate. You have let the past drive you apart. I beg you to let the past heal you. Let me share with you what I have learned over these seven weeks. Let me share with all of you what each of you have shared with me."

Stan lifts two large books, pressed together between his two large hands. He places them on the table in front of him, and leans forward, resting both his hands upon them, "The past is your foundation. The past is your cornerstone. And if you destroy the cornerstones of your beliefs, at the very most—-all you have is a struggle for meaning. And within that struggle, you make up a reason why death is not only unavoidable, but that makes it preferable. You've used the past to destroy, rather than to heal. And you've destroyed the light in your children's eyes."

Suddenly, the lights go out. Gasps are heard throughout the room. It catches everyone by surprise. They sit in darkness.

A startling image appears in the darkness as a light shines beneath Stan's face, a flashlight held under his chin, "And all they see is an unclear vision of your face. Our children's eyes see no light shed upon any foundation. And they can no longer see the true light seen through the founding fathers' eyes."

The lights go back on.

Stan sets the flashlight on the floor, and rests his hands upon the books on the table in front of him, "The founding fathers of what you believe, your patriarchs, did not lead you to peace. But neither did they direct you to war. Take Abraham, for instance, he dearly loved both his children. But he could not find peace in his own household. There was great strife. We cannot read of the account without feeling the pain, without feeling the hurt. But we've taken that hurt and created that as our banner. We've become so all consumed in our hurt that we fail to read on. We fail to read on about the healing that was supposed to have already taken place. The hurt was passed on, but the healing was not. When Abraham died, Ishmael and Isaac, with the common bond of the love of their father, joined together for Abraham's burial. They buried their differences for that brief moment. They reconciled. But did the reconciliation pass on, or did the hurt? Isaac's two sons, Esau and Jacob took a long time to find peace, even within themselves. Esau went to Ishmael's people to find a wife. Jacob tried working seven years for a wife, yet found the seven years would not reveal that which he had hoped for."

One of the men rises slowly, "It is true. I have carried my hatred too long. I would, that my son would die, before I would part with my anger and my hatred. But I will stand up and confess my error to my people. As Ishmael and Isaac joined together to bury their father, I will bury my differences. I have stood against my own son, my only son, because of his desire to marry one whom I am not willing to accept. And I stand before you today, with no reason, other than pride, to stand in the way. So, as Jacob gave seven years of work, I am willing to turn our seven weeks of seven days,—-into seven years. I would like all of you here to believe that we can extend our seven weeks into seven years of peace. And then why not seventy times seven, and save our children's children's children. Let us begin this peace agreement with a celebration of my son's wedding. Let me now return unto my son to give him my blessing. Let us celebrate together in giving all of our children the blessing they so desperately deserve—-the blessing of peace—-not the vile curse we have given them through war."

****

It was a slow and difficult process, but they had finally negotiated what most would consider—-world peace. Peace in the Middle East, that is.

Stan was known for his computer prowess. But not all had recognized his effective charismatic appeal, and the respect he drew from it ...though none could deny it now. And few would think he'd return to the small walled community, especially now after having conquered the world per se.

George and Stan Olitz were two names that would never be forgotten in all of history. But they were not too lofty for Fernye's prayers. Her prayers were spoken to the One who can conquer all things. And she'd have a thing or two to say about it too.

George and Stan had more or less established a second home in Jerusalem. Rebekkah had visited them there several times, and upon returning home, she continued to keep in touch on a weekly basis. But shortly after the peace agreement, she took ill.

The convenient overseas communication would no longer suffice. After all, Rebekkah had been a lifetime friend of George. And George wanted to be by her side.

The reason why they returned to the walled community didn't matter to Fernye. She thanked God for answering her prayers.

George said Rebekkah could count on him ...and he was not about to leave anytime soon. Fernye figured that meant she could count on Stan to be around also. As father and son, George and Stan were inseparable.

When George arrives at the hospital room, all other visitors decide to step out for a bite to eat—-leaving George and Rebekkah alone.

George leans over the hospital bed, and kisses Rebekkah on the forehead, "You're still strong as a bull."

Rebekkah counters, "I'll soon be ninety. It's not often that they even attempt open-heart surgery on someone my age."

George continues to hold her hand, "They're not dealing with your typical person here. You're one of a kind. And the medical advances have been significant in the past few years."

Rebekkah squeezes his hand, "Does anyone trust the medical field has advanced enough for someone advanced in age like me?"

George gently rests his other hand on their clasped hands, "We've been through worse ...you know we have. I know no other person on earth with a stronger will than you."

Rebekkah looks out the window, "My strong 'will' has not always served me well. Let's hope that this time it does." She looks into George's eyes, "Thanks for being my friend."

George looks into Rebekkah's soft eyes, "Thanks for being my friend too."

Rebekkah's eyes soften, forming a single tear in each eye, "It's been way too easy for me. You're the one who has been a true friend, watching after me all these years. You've always given your all ....and I often regret that I haven't."

George lifts her hand, kissing it, "Now, now, let's not make your heart too heavy. It will need plenty of rest for tomorrow."

Rebekkah feels powerless against her thoughts, "I was always afraid I'd make a mistake. And in fear of making a mistake, I've perhaps made my biggest."

George now invites the thought, "What mistake was that?"

Rebekkah chokes out the words, holding back the tears, "I believe I was wrong in not marrying you." She releases a breath with a soft laugh, "But you were wrong too."

George sits on the bed beside her, leaning on one arm, stretched out across her, "How's that?"

Rebekkah smiles, "You said you needed help in raising Stan. Well, you were wrong. You've done a fine job, all by yourself. No one can take that from you."

George straightens up and again clasps Rebekkah's hand in both of his, "So, it's settled then?"

Rebekkah's voice rises a bit above a whisper, "What's settled?"

"Will you marry me?" George slips off the bed. At first it appears as if he's dropping to one knee to propose to her. But Rebekkah soon realizes it's not that at all. George falls completely backwards, and strikes his head.

George quickly gets back up, insisting he's okay. But, Rebekkah had already pushed the nurse's button.

Rebekkah sits up in bed, "No, you're not okay. And you have a nasty bump there." She grabs the handkerchief from George's own jacket front pocket and dabs at a small accumulation of blood beginning to trickle from the quickly rising bump.

George almost falls again. Again, Rebekkah presses the nurse's button for assistance ...but no need, as a nurse rushes into the room, and steadies George to prevent the second fall.

George is unknowingly resistive. He is mumbling something. Some words can be made out, others run together—-none of it making clear sense, but Rebekkah attempts to listen. What is he saying? Is it thanks, or franks? Food-man, or good man? Never cold, or never told?

It almost sounded like George was having both sides of this conversation, and thanking her for referring to him as a 'good man'—-while venting his own frustrations of her having never let him know, never telling him that she loved him—-'never told'.

No, that was more like the thoughts she was having. He had smashed his head rather hard. He was having scrambled brain activity. Garbled, it sounded like he wanted a hotdog from a food-man. George liked to go to baseball games. And he always said the franks at the ballpark were the best. He keeps repeating it ...and each time it sounds slightly different.

Rebekkah hopes she had not put too much pressure on George's heart. He had flattered her by commenting on how well she was doing for her age, but he is a couple years older than she is. George certainly does not look his age, but you have to wonder if he's been doing too much.

****

Stan postpones his appointment with the media until after he is certain George is okay. He then reschedules it, inviting the media to the walled community.

With cameras rolling, the media inquires, "So, the burning question still remains, Stan. How did you get them to agree to peace?"

Stan had chosen the main dining area of the community church as the interview site. He takes a bite of a hotdog, swallows, then wipes his mouth with a napkin, "Oh, it was nothing. You just have to be at the right place at the right time. They've perhaps been the most misunderstood people of all time. They are truly a loving people—-all of them. Everyone wanted the peace—-they just had to be guided into it."

The camera quickly pans the cozy atmosphere of the dining area before posing the next question, "So, what would you say is next on your agenda, Stan—-having now accomplished world peace?"

Stan takes a large bite and speaks with his mouth full, "World hunger."

Everyone at the table laughs, as well as the media—-who've already planned their next comments, "Well, I guess they say that peace begins at home. So perhaps the same could be said for curing hunger. But seriously, do you have a plan in place for curing world hunger?"

Stan wipes his mouth and swallows, "I don't, but my friend Shannon here has been working on one."

Stan turns to Shannon, "Would you like to share with them what you told me yesterday?"

Shannon is rather surprised and unprepared to say anything, but the camera is now upon her. She does her best to hide her embarrassment.

Stan saves her, "Well, Shannon and I were discussing how some of the developments of capitalism do not always serve us best. We've always viewed a competitive market to be a healthy one, but at times our striving to be competitive on so many varied levels, actually does not maximize our productivity. Sometimes, even in our individual lives, we can become quite non-productive by focusing on too many things at once."

Stan takes a smaller bite of hotdog, "So, Shannon brought it to my attention that if we'd focus on just a half dozen struggling third-world countries—-to help them out, by allowing them to focus on producing just one thing—-then they could achieve more maximum productivity. Her suggestion was that we take those half dozen countries, and have them focus exclusively on the production of bread. Then they could distribute the bread throughout the world, and there would be no more hunger."

The media supplies the question that perhaps all of the viewing audience at home would be asking, "But wouldn't the burden of distribution be difficult, and perhaps far exceed even the cost of production? Who would handle the distribution?"

Stan smiles, "You know, that is the same question I'd asked Shannon. And she said that would be taken care of by donations."

Shannon, with her wonderful classic laugh, cannot contain herself.

Stan joins in on the laughter, "I was, at first, taken by the concept. But it's the only way to go. Such a charitable thing would obviously have to be taken care of by donations."

Stan pauses before repeating, "Dough nations?"

Stan believes in a healthy mix of both humor and seriousness. Maybe he should end on a serious note, but Stan also likes the 'old one-two', "But, we want nations to do more than just survive ...we want them to thrive. And most of all we want them to be happy. Isn't that right, Shannon?"

Shannon, by this time, had composed herself, "Happiness is good." Though she feels happiness in the wrong area is not good.

Stan takes on a very serious look, "Most problems in the world come from the fact that most people are not really happy. So, my recommendation is to do more than just have 'embassies'. To end unhappiness in the world, we should set up stations in every locale, town, or village ...and I favor ice cream cone stands to 'lick' that problem."

Shannon looks over at Stan, rolls her eyes, and smiles. She had laughed herself out with Stan's first joke, yet she tries to be polite.

It seems petty to discuss it, so she won't, but she wonders if Stan really believes that being happy is most important. Or was he solely going for the laugh. Grandma had said that Stan had not appeared happy for a long time, yet just in the past few years he'd been opening up more and enjoying life. And no one can argue the seriousness of the peace he just helped bring about while he was in the Middle East. Stan could afford some relaxation and 'happy time!. As Grandma would always say, "As long as it doesn't conflict with eternal happiness."

Time to lighten up, like Stan has done, and don't make something out of nothing. Only God can do that. There, she has just used a play on words ...in her own head, anyway. Unlike Stan, she can't do it with the cameras rolling. Stan has come a long way. He is amazing!

XXVIII.

Everyone is amazed that Rebekkah is so quickly out of surgery and doing so well.

Everyone ...except, Fernye.

Fernye is an extraordinary person herself. Occasionally she wouldn't feel well, but she'd usually get over it in a day or two with a little rest. It's simply amazing that she never has any real health problems, and she's 23 years Rebekkah's senior.

Rebekkah thanks Fernye for being by her side. Fernye is a true warrior—-a prayer warrior, that is—-praying Rebekkah through surgery.

And Fernye is also persistent with nagging George about his appointments. More tests are forthcoming with George. It's not conclusive what's really ailing him. They'll have to wait for the tests to reveal more. Meanwhile, according to Fernye, hopefully George will learn the difference between caring and nagging, stating how typical it often is for men to 'cop an attitude' to avoid taking full responsibility for themselves.

With all that, Fernye is not so busy that she can't keep her dream alive. She continues to pray for Stan and Shannon. But her quick assessment is that those prayers are not doing as well.

That's Fernye's emotional response though. Through all her years of prayer, she knows full well that often things aren't what or where they appear to be. And her conviction is that if you pray, and then work real hard to make the prayer come true, it's not showing lack of faith as long as you give God all the credit when it does come true.

Most people didn't know quite what Fernye meant when she said God prefers fruits to vegetables. But she was not about to sit around. God gladly gives us the fruits of our labors, she'd say. And no one could deny the blessings that came to and from Fernye.

She always wanted to share whatever blessings—-whether her own or someone else's. She always said that someone else's blessing is always our own also. We should have as much joy for each other as for ourselves.

That all soon becomes evident at the celebration of Fernye's 113th birthday. Fernye teases, "I didn't think you were celebrating my 113th birthday. I thought you were bringing recognition to a much loftier achievement. Today is the opening of our 113th walled community, nationally. And by this time next year, that number is supposed to more than double."

The concept of the walled community had started slow, but now is really catching on. Several times a year, conferences are held to explain the concept, and tours are held in already established walled communities. It is fitting to celebrate a true blessing. The Metamora community feels especially blessed this day.

George and Rebekkah are each doing much better. And of course, the main focus is the celebration of the oldest person in America. But Stan temporarily steals the spotlight.

Stan's awkward delivery of his announcement brings most of the smiles. He had so eloquently helped negotiate peace in the Middle East, yet he is stammering through the words now, not knowing quite what's proper under these circumstances, nor really how to go about saying what he wants to say, "I know I'm supposed to ask someone's permission. And as ill-equipped as I am at this, I do have some knowledge—-enough to know that I'm supposed to ask Shannon's dad, and I would've. But since that's not possible, I'm asking all of you." Stan is doing okay at it now. It just takes him a moment to talk through his nervousness, "I'm asking you—-my community, my support, my loved ones—-permission to court Shannon, with intent to marry."

Shannon likes Stan, but this throws her totally off guard. Stan had said he *would've* asked her dad, but the <u>*would've*</u> didn't help her much now. Dad *would've* insisted that Stan be more discreet. If Stan *would've* talked to him privately, Dad *would've* asked if the two of them had already discussed this ...and her feelings *would've* been considered before anyone *would've* known of Stan's intent.

But now, Shannon's feelings are all over the map. She doesn't really want to escape. She just wants time. And though the idea of courtship is supposed to provide for that very thing, she feels that perhaps Moriah's invitation had already mapped out the better solution. Just last week, Moriah had once again extended the invitation. She is to join her parents on another mission trip. And once again she'd invited Shannon to go along.

Shannon had been excited, as usual. Though she's twenty-eight years old, she still goes to Mom for advice. And of course, Mom had her usual way of expressing herself. Though she can't tell her she is too young anymore, she'd voiced her wishes that she not go.

Fernye had tried to stay out of it. Anyone else, she'd be excited for, but this was different. She'd been praying for Shannon and Stan to get together. And she had rationalized in her mind that with an uncivilized people and the unpredictability factor, it was no place for Shannon. All considered, it is a fine thing to bring the gospel to far-reaching places. But let Shannon do some other fine thing right here—-like deciding to marry Stan.

Only Mom and Fernye had actually heard Shannon mention the Indonesian trip, and the fact that she didn't talk about it again sort of seemed like she'd decided not to go. That's why it takes everyone by surprise now, "Stan, I'm going to be going on the mission trip with Moriah and her parents next week. Could you please pray for me about that?" Everyone falls silent. Shannon feels extremely awkward, "I'm not going away for—-forever. It is only a one year commitment."

****

Cindy waits until the morning. Shannon always wakes up earlier than the rest, and is sitting, curled up against the arm of the sofa. Cindy snuggles up beside her, "Why are you really going to the mission field?"

Shannon tries to find the words, "Sometimes in life, we just have to try what we've been avoiding. But this isn't like mountain climbing, or skydiving—-nothing like that. This is mission work."

Cindy is not convinced, "Or are you trading one thing for another? I've been avoiding the idea of you going to the mission field, but you're avoiding the thought that you and Stan could have a good life together. Does trying what you've been avoiding include giving you and Stan a try? When you were fourteen, you said you'd never marry. I was fine with that. I didn't want you to think of courtship and marriage at such a young age. And at that time the answer would have been unquestionably, *"No!"* But now you are old enough to say, *"Yes!"* I don't have a problem with you following God's *will* for your life ...I just think it may be right here?"

Shannon is feeling the burden of painful decision-making, "Please, try to understand, Mom. You've had a chance to live out a few of your dreams. And lately you all have tried to live out Dad's dreams. That's fine, but I have to find my own dreams too."

Cindy passes her concern on ...and Fernye takes a turn, "So, you're trying to find your dream. Have you prayed about it?"

Shannon is hesitant in mentioning this, but the pressure of keeping it inside is too great, "I prayed that I'd stop having the dream."

Fernye offers advice instead of a question, "What if God gives you a dream? It wouldn't be right to pray against it."

Shannon offers a question, "Grandma, how do you suppose Job's friends got to be the way they were?"

Grandma doesn't understand the correlation. She can't imagine Shannon would compare Stan to one of Job's friends, but Fernye is always willing to share her wisdom, "Well, they appeared to be good men, filled with the knowledge of God. But they appeared to get to a point where they viewed wisdom as a *one size fits all* solution. We shouldn't perceive ourselves so wise that we dispense wisdom on our own, instead of returning to where the wisdom first came from. If we don't get that right, a confusion can breed, and it is difficult to discern what is God's wisdom and what is our own. If we take a circumstance that God has guided us through in the past and attempt to apply it to someone else's circumstance, we may be overlooking what God would have us see. That is our own wisdom. God's wisdom is for our unique situation, and we are not wise enough to know the personalized nature of it. And others may not seek out God if we portray to others that we and wisdom are one and the same."

Shannon returns to her previous mention, "How do you know whether a dream comes from God? I keep having this dream that Dad is crying, and I wake up crying in the night."

Fernye explains, "That is really common. It usually means you have unresolved emotions concerning something. You know, while Dad was here, you had never really shown Dad that you accepted him. So it could be that those emotions are pouring out in your dreams."

Shannon is still confused, "But why is Stan in my dreams? My dreams have Dad crying and me crying, but Stan never cries."

Fernye smiles, "Maybe you do care about Stan more than you'd like to admit. And the emotions you were holding back from Dad, you are now holding back with Stan. That's a common transference. In your case, it would be emotional guardedness."

Shannon would like to feel confident about what God would have her see in this whole emotional entanglement, "But it's not just a dream, Grandma. I've never seen Stan cry, for real."

Fernye tries to share the wisdom of her past experiences, "Well, that's because men are simply not brought up to cry. That's always the way it was, and for the most part it probably will never change. Thankfully, they are brought up to be sensitive to our crying. But don't expect them to cry."

Shannon is searching, "Even when they're boys, they learn not to cry?"

Fernye affirms, "That's precisely when they learn. It's a sad time, especially for mothers. They dread to see the day their sons turn from hugging and kissing them—-to portraying a rough exterior."

Shannon's heart begs to differ, "But not all of them do. I saw Dad cry lots of times."

Fernye appears so focused on defending Stan, she forgets her past fondness of Stephen, "Well, when a man cries too much, what does a woman have left to do? If there's one thing a woman can't stand, it's being upstaged when she feels like crying."

Shannon feels this is an outcry of injustice. That's one of the many things she feels is so special—-when a man doesn't bend to expectations. Dad was special that way. And no one can change her perception of him.

Fernye continues though, "When a man and woman happen to switch roles—-well, that's what happened with the *women's liberation movement*."

Shannon wonders what happened to Grandma. She always seemed to know what to say, and it was refreshing to see God working through her, but why doesn't Shannon feel that way now? Is it because Fernye is getting old? No, that's ridiculous. She's way past *getting*,—-it's just that she can be so right-on, then other times, she just sounds like the rest of society.

Shannon just has to ask, "So, what happened with the *women's liberation movement*? Did the men all start crying?"

Shannon recalls Grandma saying the movement was a crying shame.

But Fernye appears tired, so she doesn't respond with her usual humor "Well, no. Most of the men didn't do anything. So naturally, the women had to."

Shannon sees it *this* way, "Dad and Mom didn't switch roles."

Fernye sees it *another* way, but doesn't choose to bring up that point, "Well, maybe not, but your Mom has to do both roles now. She's had to for several years now. You'd make it easier on her if you'd marry Stan. All the Christ-like character that any woman could ever look for in a man ...well, that's Stan. You'll find no better."

Fernye is so convinced that the best thing for Shannon is Stan. So much so, that she can't help add, "Yes, your Dad was a good man, but your Mom told me some things. I'm sorry to say, he was a bit insecure. And I believe that's why you saw him cry. Stan is a very secure young man. I believe he has the joy of walking with God. You probably don't see him cry, but I'd find no fault with that. You'll find more happiness sharing joy, than tears."

Shannon is emotionally exhausted, "Yes, perhaps you're right, Grandma. I'm just confused about a lot of stuff at this stage of my life. But just one more thing—-could you explain to me one more thing?"

Grandma feels she has made her point, "Sure, what is it?"

Shannon asks, "In the Gospel of John, what does Chapter eleven, verse thirty-five mean?"

XXIX.

Fernye says she feels a heaviness in her chest. Cindy says she has the same heaviness of heart, now that Shannon is gone. But Fernye insists that it's not the same. So to be on the safe side, Cindy agrees to take her to the hospital for a checkup.

Cindy stares ahead at the road. She does not say much. She really can't believe Shannon is gone—-but she is.

Fernye isn't saying much either. She just gazes out the car window. Suddenly, Fernye hollers, "Turn back!"

Cindy immediately senses danger at the tone of the command, "What! What's the matter?"

Fernye insists, "Just turn back!"

Cindy quickly turns on her directional signal and turns on the first street to the left, "Okay. Now where and what am I turning back to?"

Fernye has calmed down a bit, but still has an anxious tone, "Just drive, I'll tell you when to stop!"

Cindy drives back a quarter mile. Fernye then cautions, "Slow down a bit—-get ready to pull off. Okay, right here!"

Cindy pulls off, "Okay, what is it?"

Fernye's heart leaps for joy, "Don't you see it?"

Cindy looks, "I see a barren field. You are looking here to the right, aren't you?" Fernye continues her ecstatic joy, "It's a field full of golden wheat, ready for harvest!"

Cindy looks to Fernye, then back out the window, "I'm sorry, Grandma, I still see a barren field. The sun is shining, perhaps casting a slight golden hue across the surface of the field. But I still just see a barren field."

Cindy is glad they're going to the hospital. For a 113 year old, she's still sharp. But it's time for a check-up, for sure.

Fernye turns to Cindy, "Don't you see? I tried to convince Shannon not to go, but I believe I was wrong. She did the right thing. I somehow feel good about it now. There is a barren field out there—-barren of the truth of Jesus. And Shannon is going to help plant, cultivate, and witness a golden harvest. Can you see it now?"

Cindy smiles, "Yes, I see it now! And I guess I should've set my emotions aside too. And yes, I know God takes care of us all—-and certainly He will guide those who are most willing to let Him guide them."

Fernye smiles, "If you put another person's needs before your own, you meet two people's needs. If you put your own needs first, you meet no one's needs."

Cindy laughs, "Why are we going to the hospital, Grandma? You're as healthy as you've ever been."

Fernye chuckles, "We're not going to a spiritual counselor. My body is old. You bring your car in for a tune-up every so often, don't you?"

Cindy pulls back around, and proceeds to drive to the hospital.

Fernye seems to drift in thought, but chooses to share those thoughts, "Shannon was ready to grow. She wasn't ready to cultivate a relationship with Stan. If you cultivate before the growth begins, you just uproot that growth. Stan felt a need to be with someone, and that someone at this time was Shannon. But that would be putting his own needs, or what he felt were his needs, first. And as I said, then you meet no one's needs. Stan has gone through so much. He has matured. But we've sheltered Shannon. We've attempted to shelter her from things we felt that were not good, but we can't also shelter her from what is good. This mission experience is good. And Stan is good. When she returns, she'll be much more mature. She'll be ready to meet Stan on his level. Just wait and see."

****

There is the fear of love realized too soon, and the fear of love not realized. The latter is the case with George. Instead of talking about marriage, Rebekkah had asked to be courted.

Hand-delivering flowers, he modifies his voice in a comical fashion, adding a drawl to his slowed speech, "I've heard our dear friend, Fernye, say over and over again—-that you can sure catch more flies with honey than vinegar. Now, we all know honey comes from a flower and a bee, so these flowers be—-for you."

Rebekkah holds back her laugh, attempting to maintain at least a semi-serious tone, "Oh, how romantic, George! I've considered myself many things—-but a fly, to be caught? What tangled web you weave! But, of course, you're quoting Fernye, so I understand it's not intended to be anything, but old folk romantic. Next, I expect you'll say my hair is like corn silk—-and it glistens like dew on the morning grass."

****

Rebekkah returns to visit George that evening within his humble little dwelling. George is a refreshing part of the walled community. He is scheduled for surgery later in the week. They had discovered a tumor, the size of a fist, in the back of his head. It seems to rain on the *just and the unjust*. The same thing had happened to Ruth's dad ...there was nothing 'just' about him. But, George is such a good man ...and a dear friend.

Rebekkah knocks at his door. Most everyone in the community felt safe and secure enough to not worry about locking their door, but George said the reason he continues to lock his door is that he needs uninterrupted concentration to conduct his business.

Being a CEO of a business is not a carefree endeavor. When he was younger, it didn't bother him as much. But now he sometimes needs the added solitude. Still, there is none better than him at running a business. Stan is the best when it comes to computers, but he doesn't have the business sense of George. Though Stan is being groomed by George. One day, Stan will have learned all that business savvy.

Rebekkah knocks again, certain he said he'd be expecting her at this time. But maybe she should wait a minute or two, allowing him time to finish his task.

Instinctively, she tries the door. It is unlocked!

It is not like George to not answer the door, and even more unlike him to leave the door unlocked. Well, he was expecting her, but still, she senses something is wrong.

As she enters, her heartbeat is racing. She finds George at his computer. But George does not look right. Something is wrong!

Rebekkah slowly moves around, behind George. His finger is poised, as if ready to proceed on the computer. She glances momentarily at the computer screen.

Suddenly, he taps one last letter of an access code. George's hand is once again frozen in position just above the keyboard. Something is definitely wrong! He appears to be in some sort of trance. Her guess is that perhaps he's having a stroke. She has no medical knowledge, but she needs to call an ambulance.

George's hand drops, striking the ENTER key. Then his head drops to the side as his body becomes limp, slumping in his chair.

She attempts to support him the best she can, enduring the added weight as she lowers him safely to the floor, without allowing him to strike his head.

****

Stan paces back and forth outside the operating room. He hopes it's not too late. They had rushed George into surgery. He just hopes they were in time. But he is not alone with this hope of his. Many are in prayer.

The Doctors are confident after surgery. They speak hopeful words. They reassure Stan, and the rest of the prayer group, that they believe they didn't destroy any of the area around the tumor. They are hopeful he'll be himself again. But they'll be more certain in a couple days.

****

In a short time, George shows much improvement. Of course, one's physical health is important ..as it keeps us alive. Once a patient is improving physically, there is an assessment as to whether the patient is mentally stable. George seems to be doing well.

Yet, how is a person's health evaluated when the person is not hospitalized, and actually it is not really even a consideration? How about a person who hides their problems ...especially the type of problems that would be difficult to evaluate?

Shannon is in great physical health. Nothing really to worry about there. But, she is very unsettled. She has been in the mission field less than a month, but sadly it already seems so long ...and perhaps wrong, for her. Had she chosen wisely?

Shannon does not let on that she is not doing well though. She calls home, and listens to all the news Mom has to share. She had committed to one year in the Indonesian mission field. And she isn't about to go back on that commitment.

As Shannon gets off the phone with Mom, she cries.

She could tell Mom was crying while she was on the phone. But Shannon didn't let on like she was having a miserable time. She misses Mom so much—-and Leah, Josiah, and Samuel. But there's more to it than that. She misses Dad too.

Being out in the mission field has much potential joy, but Shannon is yet to experience that. There is also a certain sense of being somewhat scared—-not knowing what to do. She recalls that Dad had always fixed things—-or had attempted to. Dad had never seemed to be able to fix it with Mom, but even when things seemed out-of-control, in a sort of way, Dad gave a secure feeling that he was at least struggling to attempt to make things right—-even if in an unpeaceful way.

In a strange sort of way, it was still peaceful when Dad was involved in her thoughts. He may have been wrong in the way he often had done things, but at least he'd struggled for what he wanted to make right.

And Shannon finds that admirable. It brings a deep sense of peace. Dad had a fault of perhaps worrying too much, but he was concerned ...and who could fault him for caring too much? Dad probably wouldn't have even let her go to the mission field. Grandma and Mom had discouraged her, but Dad would have done more—-he wouldn't have let her go to this strange far away place.

Shannon feels the warmth of Dad's arms around her. It is strange. She had never allowed that warmth, but now as she imagines it—-it feels so good. Yes, this is strange. Dad has been gone for over fifteen long years now—-and it has taken this long to be able to feel this kind of peace.

The strange feeling now engulfs her, and sweeps her along to imaginings she had not expected. As she imagines Dad's arms wrapped around her, the image suddenly becomes ...Stan.

It is like she suddenly wants a hug from Stan. She and Stan had never hugged, held hands, or anything for that matter—-but suddenly she feels Stan's love—-the way she feels Dad's love. She'd been unprepared for this emotional journey, but as it unfolds before her, she begins to feel she even understands part of it.

In a way, an allowance is being made for an emotion that had been hindered, without any previous avenue for growth. Is that the way life goes?

Unexplainable? Not really ...it's been happening ever since the beginning of time. It merely happens because it is supposed to happen. It's not really as unexplainable as one may think—-it's God's way. She just hasn't experienced this sort of thing in her life before. Maybe it just takes a little slowing down, moving out of our typical agendas, and experiencing a new perspective.

Shannon begins to laugh at herself. These feelings are probably very common ...all a part of growth and maturity. Just ask Fernye!

****

Time has a way of marching on. Shannon is nearing her year away from home. She has learned much. Often dreaming of adventures is the most fun, but she should also be experiencing what Moriah is feeling.

Shannon had always considered her cousin, Moriah, her best friend. They would forever share dreams and adventures of their imaginations. But now that the adventure is real, it does not have the same effect for Shannon. She feels a little guilty. She feels she should be experiencing the joy that Moriah is feeling. After all, what greater joy could a Christian feel than introducing Jesus to a group of people yet void of that understanding?

What Shannon clearly does understand, is that she has too many other feelings rising to the surface. Above all, she feels she has to be honest with herself. Maybe she hadn't been ready for the mission field. Maybe during a different time, she would have been able to feel the same joy that Moriah seems to be experiencing.

Moriah had told Shannon she had some of the same uncertain feelings during her first mission trip. But Shannon knew that wasn't the same. There is usually a sense of uneasiness that comes with experiencing new things, but Shannon's uneasiness is with the imaginings of a different sort of journey. She had gone to the mission field, not because she had been drawn to it, but because she was drawing herself away ...from any closeness that Stan may have been feeling towards her.

****

The year is finally through! Shannon is coming home. And the very thing that she had run away from ...is now drawing her close. She misses her family so much! But her feelings had done a complete turnabout with Stan. She is no longer afraid ...and she misses him too.

She is eager to explore the adventures of her heart through courtship. She hadn't tried to nourish the thought, but the more the thought crosses her mind, the more it begins to settle in with quiet contentment, towards commitment. She wants to settle down. And she wants to settle down with someone she can love ...and who will love her. Stan had already announced both his feelings and his intentions. And Shannon feels she is ready to meet him on those terms.

Shannon says goodbye to Moriah and her parents. Moriah had committed to two years, so Shannon will be taking the trip back alone, without her cousin ...her dear friend and companion.

Shannon cries as she steps to the plane. Moriah and her mom, Aleah, cry too. But Lorvin doesn't cry. Lorvin is perhaps much like Stan. Shannon kind of laughs to herself through the tears, as she thinks back just a year ago. She had made such a big deal about not ever seeing Stan cry.

In the mission field, Shannon had seen many men void of God's leading and direction. Cultures had developed for hundreds of years without any of God's influence and understanding. Sadly, many of them reminded her of men in her own country—-a country where the vast majority had at one time believed in God, yet still, God's influence scarce to recognize. Then in the name of unity and everything that it represents—-*the Essence* had made its inroads in her own country. And with peace and acceptance as avenues to link diversity and unity, there became an acceptance of diverse beliefs in God, stripping away truth and character—-much resembling those who are void of those standards which God freely extends to us through His Son, Jesus. All this brings a new perspective to how Shannon really feels about life. And it increases her appreciation for a man such as Stan.

As Shannon gets off the plane, she looks around. She doesn't see anyone immediately. She wonders how much more disappointment she must face. Then some movement catches her eye. Mom breaks from the crowd. Shannon drops her onboard luggage, and they embrace each other.

Then some big strong arms wrap around them both. Is it Stan? She turns her head to see. It is Samuel.

Samuel reminds Shannon of Grandpa Bauer with that gentle kindness of heart, yet a certain comforting strength—-and a great strength of character. She is so happy that Samuel is here too. She teases, "Why aren't you taking care of my horse?"

Samuel smiles, "I have been. I thought that Malachi would be okay for at least a couple hours."

Shannon laughs, "I guess since he's too old to ride now, it's still no excuse for me to ride you." Giving another big hug, "I really missed you, Samuel." She finally asks, "So ...where are Leah and Josiah?"

Cindy confesses, "I know this is rather selfish of me, but I wanted to spend some time alone with you first, before everyone else floods you with questions."

Cindy hugs Shannon for a very long time, "I missed you so much, Shannon."

Cindy and Shannon sit in the back seat of the car while Samuel drives.

Shannon smiles, "So, Leah and Josiah wanted to come along, but you wouldn't let them?"

Cindy reaches out to touch Shannon's hand, "They understand how Moms are."

Shannon gently squeezes Mom's hand, then laughs, "So, where shall we start?" Samuel drives, and listens as Shannon tells Mom of her missionary experiences.

****

Rebekkah, Fernye, and Ken are next to greet Shannon as she arrives at the walled community. Shannon can't help noticing the absence of Leah and Josiah, though this just piques her anticipation. She expects they will surprise her at any moment.

Mom takes half that surprise away, "No one knew quite when you'd be arriving. And I guess it's my fault again. I was supposed to call ahead to tell them when we were arriving, but I was so eager to see you, I got carried away and forgot. Josiah should be at the printing room, off the church building. He's finishing the first 500 copies of 'The Essence'. He is so eager to see you. So is Leah, but I don't know where she is."

Shannon heads to the printing room. She looks about. She'd shared so much with Mom. But she'd not mentioned her silent wish about Stan. She is partly relieved that she has not seen him yet. She wants to see Josiah and Leah first. She might cry when she sees Stan, and it would be better if her eyes are already filled with tears.

Josiah sees Shannon coming. He runs and meets her halfway, sweeping his sister up in his arms. They both laugh and cry. It is such a joyous reunion.

Shannon asks to see the book, but Josiah says he has a copy set aside for her. "You can see it later. I'm sure Leah can't wait to see you. I think she's in the barn."

Shannon runs and skips to the barn. She is so excited. She could spend hours talking to Leah. Mom knew that, of course, and had made sure to mention that she expected them back for dinner.

Leah had shown interest in the mission field. She had wanted to go with Shannon, but Mom had told her "next time", hoping there would never be a next time. Shannon and Leah both understood that, of course. They all knew that Mom always wanted the whole family together—-and was so relieved that Shannon was now safely back home.

There are some things that Shannon is particularly eager to talk with Leah about. She will not share with anyone else how difficult it was for her in the mission field, but she will be able to share that with Leah. And she'll also share with Leah the feelings she now has towards Stan. Leah will understand. It won't remain a secret long anyway. Sometimes sisters sense these things without having to be told. She will tell Leah all about it. Leah will be so happy for her.

The excitement builds as Shannon approaches the barn. Across the front of the barn, stretching its full length, a huge banner reads: WELCOME HOME, SHANNON!!!

The barn door is open. Shannon slips inside. She can see Stan leaning against the top rail of Malachi's pen. He is facing away from her. Shannon keeps to the wall. She wants to surprise Stan.

Suddenly, Leah's voice is heard. She must be inside Malachi's pen. Stan stretches his arm out across the rail, "When I tried to announce my full intentions with your sister, a year ago, it was embarrassing. I was rather surprised ...because you know, I thought she felt the same way as I did."

Hearing this brings Shannon to tears. Then she sees something glimmer in the light, on Stan's fingers.

Leah asks, "Is that tape on your fingers, Stan?"

Suddenly, Shannon recalls the video she had taped, one of her favorites, a portion of Dad, left behind. The puppet show comes to mind:

Breeze: "You stick with her as long as she wants."

Cody: "How long does she want?"

Breeze: "Until she gets a ring on her finger instead of tape."

Overcome with emotion, more tears gather in Shannon's eyes. Stan had decided to stick with her. How long had he waited? He'd waited an entire year, not knowing her intentions. He must be so very nervous, worried that she may reject him again ...he's trying to calm himself by talking to her sister. Now he is waiting for her. This time she will surprise him ...with open arms. And he will soon give her a ring, instead of tape. This is all so endearing to her heart.

Stan's arm draws back, "I just wanted to check with you first, Leah."

Leah's voice is overcome with emotion, "This catches me a little off guard. What is this you are now saying ...with Shannon about to arrive at any moment. Are you telling me you are about to propose to her again?"

The sound of tape being peeled off a roll is heard. Stan rolls with it, "Your entire family is so special to me. Shannon made it rather clear a year ago that she was not going to accept my proposal. Having to see her again kind of makes me feel awkward. It kind of still hurts. I'd like someone who is sure they want to stand by my side. I'm just asking for you, Leah, to stick with me—-until I can get you a ring, instead of tape."

Shannon gasps for breath, trying not to make a vocal sound with the sudden intake of air. She slips back quickly along the wall. She cannot face him just yet. She has to compose herself first.

Shannon does well with composing herself. After several minutes, she knocks on the barn door, and hollers inside. The tears are there, of course. Leah rushes to her and cries with her, telling her how much she has missed her.

Several minutes pass, inclusive of Stan very politely welcoming her back. Then Josiah, having finished up at the print shop, enters the barn to remind them that it is time to eat.

While everyone is getting ready to eat, Stan announces his intentions. "I will, of course, make an announcement in church this Sunday, but you all are so very dear ...that I want to share my news with you now. I plan to marry Leah."

Shannon gives a big happy smile for her sister ...but it's also combined with a 'sadness', she truly must hide.

****

Cindy and Fernye are understandably excited, and usher Leah off to an adjacent room. It does not even register with them that they have not even eaten yet.

Leah tries to get a few words in, "This is a surprise to me. It really catches me off guard. I didn't even get a chance to tell Stan how I feel. He sort of asked, but I never even got a chance to say anything. It was so awkward ...he sprung it upon me in the barn, just before Shannon walked in."

Cindy is about to say something, but Fernye jumps in, "None of that matters, we are so happy for you. Having Stan as your husband is too much to imagine ...it would be every girl's dream. And now it's your unbelievably wonderful reality."

****

Leah does not necessarily disagree with what everyone has said about how wonderful Stan is. She has just had insufficient time to think how she personally feels.

Leah wants to have one last private moment. She takes that private moment, early in the morning, at the cemetery.

Leah drops to her knees and prays, "Oh Lord, how is a person to really know? I know the beauty of Your design points to the love of death and resurrection. I know, Lord, that You have Dad in Your loving arms. I just want to know if it's the right thing for me to be in Stan's loving arms. I guess, I'm asking You, God, if this whole thing is directed by You ...for me to marry Stan. And if so, then would You please guide this blessing that You have given to the two of us, through our courtship?" Leah can't stem back the tears, "Oh, God, I don't really know why You took my Dad away. I know You are taking good care of him, but I miss him. I always miss him. But for some reason, I miss him more now."

Leah lowers her head to rest upon clasped hands. Her tears find their way to the earth around the gravestone. She hasn't cried like this in a long time.

After quite some time, Leah stands up and begins to pace back and forth in front of the gravesite, "Okay, Dad, I know it's the proper thing to do—-to ask you for your approval and blessing. Well, I don't really know what to say. Stan is a lot like you, Dad. Some people say he's even better than you, but in my heart there will never be anyone quite like you. You are my Dad, and I know no one could love me and take care of me like you did—-except God. So, if you are convinced that Stan is God's choice for me, then I know you'll approve of me getting a ring—-an unending circle of unending love and commitment. Those are your own words, and if I could, I'd request one last dance with you—-on my wedding day. I just wish you could hold me in your arms ...and sing to me, one more time."

XXX.

Shannon has to adjust to the idea of her sister marrying Stan. If it can't be her, she'd want it to be Leah. She wants the best for her sister. Maybe it's best that it's Leah.

Shannon doesn't have much time to 'think out' her emotions. The very next morning, her beloved Appaloosa, Malachi, dies.

For whatever reasons, many that they can be, Shannon decides she is going to go back to the mission field to finish out the second year with Moriah.

This is a shock to everyone, but Shannon is certain this is what she wants to do. She assures Leah that she will be back in plenty of time for her wedding.

Leah hands Shannon her well-preserved Cody Komodo, "Here, take this with you, and think of me. I'll be praying for you. I hear there are Komodo dragons on some of those islands. I pray you'll be safe. Take care of Cody—-and remember, I'm praying for you."

****

Shannon's departure is much sooner than expected. They are all surprised at the news of her return to Indonesia, though Rebekkah had a surprise that she's confident would change Shannon's mind ...but it arrives a day too late.

They all agree that Shannon had made the decision abruptly. But, for Fernye, it is more than that ...she feels she knows why. And she feels bad that she'd not been a bit more perceptive.

When Rebekkah goes to bed, she cannot sleep. She is quite familiar with emotional torment ...but that regret is her own. Daily, she considers her own wrong decision, yet she feels paralyzed to correct it.

She considers the life Ruth had …how she had experienced what it is like, but not had any regrets. Ruth had made a decision partly out of fear …but mostly out of love. Rebekkah cannot deny her own decision was mostly out of fear. And the guilt of not pursuing that love, torments her.

Shannon had made the best decision of all. Fernye had shared her thoughts with Rebekkah …and Rebekkah feels Fernye is likely correct. Shannon had made her decision out of love. Of course, they'd never want Leah to catch wind of their suspicions. Leah was not to know …as that would not only crush her love, but affect everyone. And she'd probably never suspect anything, as long as no one told her. The entire community is stoking the fires of love …and often love is blind.

Rebekkah recalls what Fernye had said just over a year ago …that Shannon cared about Stan, but wasn't quite ready. Fernye had been confident it would happen in God's time. Rebekkah had agreed with her, but where was that wisdom leading now? It had led Shannon back to the mission field. And it appeared that she was running away.

Rebekkah had hoped to convince her that there was another way. She had hoped that her gift would convince Shannon to stay.

Meanwhile, Cindy doesn't just want to suppose she knows what is wrong, she wants to at least attempt to verify it. Maybe Leah will know something. The age difference between the two appeared significant, until the past few years. They've since become real close. Leah had always wanted to do things with her big sister, always having to be told that she was too young. Shannon was always being adventurous with Moriah, which led to her journey to the mission field. But she hadn't realized how grown up Leah was becoming. Sisters are often close, sharing everything together. Maybe Shannon had told Leah something that would explain why she returned so hastily to the mission field.

Cindy inquires, "Leah, is there anything Shannon shared with you that would indicate why she would so quickly change her mind, and want to go back to the mission field?"

Leah sadly admits, "No, Mom. She didn't tell me anything, really."

****

Rebekkah is extremely upset that her gift had not arrived on time. But she will not allow that to ruin her surprise. She will send the gift to Indonesia.

Fernye is amazed, "I guess I should have learned by now, that when you set out to do something, you don't let anything get in your way."

Rebekkah gives strict directions for them to call immediately when her gift arrives. Meanwhile, she has to occupy her time. Every minute that she waits feels like forever. She doesn't want to have another emotional event to link her deep ties to the island. She can't live forever with regrets of what she could have done.

But meanwhile, at least she can occupy her thoughts and time by working a bit more on her story. It is a painful process telling her story. She can in no way bring herself to do it through a letter, or a phone call. But she must tell the story ...the entire story.

Some of the story is through the aid of a diary Ruth had left in her care. Some of the story had been told to her by Ruth. But most of it is being told through Rebekkah's own painful memories.

The title, *So Loved*, is Rebekkah's attempt at salvaging the good amongst the bad. But the story refused to end, as tragedy often visits contentment—-birthing confusion in '*The Curious Whether and How*'. Beyond this book, Rebekkah outlines the third phase of her trilogy, before even penning a line in the second story. Yes, to endure and find meaning in life, where others have failed—-to stop, and smell the roses, not to cower over past experiences of having the thorns lodged up your nose.

Rebekkah smiles as she picks out the title of the third book she plans to write. The title comes to mind as she recalls a line from a favorite poem. It speaks for those who endure, and those who endear, *'Do the Birds in the Wilderness, Not Heard, Stop Singing Their Songs?'*.

Okay, so much for titles and outlines. Real life has to emerge out of pages of sketchy notes. She will slow down a little—-and begin to relive that which she feels she truly never really lived.

Rebekkah is in the thick of her writing, when the plot thickens across the world in Indonesia. Her gift arrives, but at that precise moment they realize that Shannon isn't there. And no one seems to know where she is.

Rebekkah has one final thing to say before ending this phone conversation with Sweeney, "Well, find her! Then call me back ...and don't take your Sweeney sweet time in doing it! She can't be lost ...someone must know where she's at!"

They take more time than Rebekkah is comfortable with ...each second tormenting her more and more. The old emotions race back with a resurgence.

Only two hours have elapsed. Finally the call comes, "I'm sorry, Rebekkah. We haven't found Shannon yet, but we have a couple witnesses that say they last saw her, Moriah, and one of the Rahayu brothers out fishing. The three of them appear to be missing. But everyone is instructed not to stay out past nightfall. I will be sure to call you when they wander back."

Rebekkah finds no comfort at all in the fact that anyone would wander about—-she can't imagine anyone wandering about in those remote and uncivilized islands. Whether they wandered off or wandered back, wandering is wandering. And her imagination wanders—-wondering if Shannon and Moriah are okay.

There is a long pause, "I know you will do your best, Maggie. I'm sorry if I sound so tense."

* * * * * * *

Maggie and Stephen Tressel are both near seventy. They are the foundation of the ministries throughout the Indonesian Islands, having been working exclusively there for over 40 years. Rebekkah recalls when she'd joined in on one of the mission trips over twenty-five years ago. As an integral part of New Tribes Mission, they were a textbook study of effective ministries.

Cindy and the children are gathered around, waiting to hear any bit of good news.

Fernye emerges from prayer, giving her vote of confidence, "I have this unbelievable feeling of relief—-like something wonderful or terrible is going to happen, depending upon your perspective. I don't know if my time is near—-or if it's something else."

This serves as no relief. Rebekkah thinks about what Fernye had said. She could be in agreement—-that if her own time is near, it'd be so wonderful to be finally ushered into heaven and eternity by the hand of Jesus. But Rebekkah fears how terrible it could be for others—-being left behind to face the conditions that she recently had learned more about. Being Fernye's age, or even her own, one could anticipate that their own *end times* perhaps is approaching. Though who could be certain of what tribulations need be endured before Jesus' return.

Rebekkah fears for those she loves so much. And she struggles with trying to do all this on her own, feeling a bit like *'Buck'* from the *Left Behind* series. She needs to trust God more. It is all in His hands ...not hers.

Lorvin and Aleah must also be worried sick, as their own daughter is reported missing with Shannon. But they are there ...and they are able to do something about it.

That gives Rebekkah some comfort, knowing they will do their best. Nevertheless, Rebekkah's frustration continues to build. She is not used to sitting back, with nothing she can do about it. She is used to being in control—-of others, not of herself.

Somehow Fernye's words always seem to penetrate the mind and lodge themselves in one's memory. Rebekkah recalls Fernye's words, "It's when you feel the most helpless ...that you are, in fact, the most help."

She knows Fernye is right—-and she sits down to pray.

* * * * * *** * *** * * * * *

Back in Indonesia, everyone is now organizing as quickly as can be expected. Feleti Rahayu says that his younger brother Hola has been mumbling lately about how he can be as effective as anyone. For the past dozen years, Feleti has been the primary translator and sole guide for Stephen and Maggie.

Hola has seemed to take a fondness to Moriah. Feleti doesn't know quite why, but he feels uncomfortable about this. He feels his younger brother might set out to try to prove something. And though Shannon and Moriah may have initially set out to sea for a relaxing break from the routine, an afternoon of fishing—-in Hola's eyes it may have become an intentional drift to another island, to attempt to become a 'fisher of men'.

Feleti fears that may be precisely what had happened, and he takes responsibility to take care of it ...his brother being involved. He prepares to set sail alone, but Sweeney and Murray claim that their ship is faster. And they also still have that issue of Shannon's gift that they have to deal with. They are expected to personally deliver the gift to Shannon, and they'd pledged to stay until that mission is fulfilled. And of course, Lorvin and Aleah insist on going.

The five person crew quickly boards the ship. Stephen and Maggie had established a base on a small island in the Lesser Sunda Islands. It is north of Sumbawa and Flores Island. Feleti *focuses in on* a small island to the north, as he directs Murray and Sweeney to set sail. Feleti has a feeling which island Hola would have chosen to sail to.

Lorvin is worried. Every minute that his daughter and Shannon are away, fills him with mounting anxiety. He considers it just briefly, then appeals, "I'm sorry, but I cannot travel to an island guided by just a feeling. Nor do I want to be guided by worry. Let's pray about this."

Feleti agrees. Prayer is the better course. Murray shuts the engine off, and lets their craft drift. Feleti doesn't wait to see who will lead the prayer, "O Lord God, please guide us the way ..."

A desperate cry penetrates their prayer, "Wait! Wait!"

The voice is that of a young man, losing ground or taking on more water, as he desperately attempts to swim to the ship.

Feleti hollers out, "Kakau!"

They turn the ship around to rescue Kakau.

Kakau crawls on board, with their help, bringing the crew to six members now. Pants and hair dripping, Kakau attempts to explain, "I didn't want to holler from the shore because you might have thought I was just a madman hollering from shore."

Feleti adds, "You're right. A drowning man certainly draws closer attention."

Kakau takes a deep breath, "I ran from the other side of the island when I heard Shannon and Moriah were missing. I saw which way Hola went with them."

Feleti smiles, "I'm glad we prayed. Kakau is a good swimmer, but I don't think he would have caught us if we had not stopped the motor to pray."

It seems to take forever, but soon they circle around to the other side of the island and sail South, which they now assume is the correct direction.

Lorvin stares out across the water. The island they had left is now out-of-sight and there is no land to be seen. The others resume praying again, but Lorvin remains silent, away from the group. He stares out over the waters, for what seems like hours.

Suddenly, Lorvin shouts, "I see something! It's ...a boat!" He wants to shout that it's them, but there is no way of knowing.

Sweeney hands Feleti a telescope. Feleti quickly identifies, "It's Folau. No one knows these islands like Folau. He's been the self-proclaimed king of these waters for the past thirty years."

Again, Lorvin is not comforted by any proclamation short of announcing where his daughter and Shannon are. As they approach Folau's vessel, Lorvin shouts another announcement, "There's land! I see land!"

Feleti is not king of the islands, but he is familiar enough, "That's Komodo Island."

As they approach Folau's vessel, Feleti suddenly begins shouting conversation that only Folau ...and those onboard his fishing vessel understand.

They number nearly a dozen, casting nets off Folau's vessel. Suddenly, a voice that can be understood brings Aleah to Lorvin's arms, and tears to both, "Hola not go Komodo Island ...Hola go there!"

The young man by the name of Malu, points, but Lorvin does not see anything. Sweeney hands him the telescope. Lorvin sees a faint, but certain silhouette of an island.

Malu climbs onboard, numbering their crew at seven. Malu talks broken English as well as most of the Islanders—-not as well as Feleti or Kakau, but well enough to understand.

Malu describes the people on the island where he said he saw Hola go. But what he says causes great concern, especially to Lorvin and Aleah. Malu says there are two islands. One island is inhabited by women and children—-the other one, only by men.

Feleti turns to Lorvin to joke, "Kind of like the Bible College you told me about—-where the men and women are expected to sit arm's length apart. But here, they sit islands apart."

Lorvin doesn't laugh. From what Malu says, Hola brought Moriah and Shannon to the men's island ...where the women are forbidden.

Lorvin asks, "What happens if a woman by chance does go to the men's island?"

Malu's answer is straightforward, "Don't know ...never happen."

Malu and Feleti continue to talk. Apparently, whenever a man dies, the chosen one by that man, if he be a 'cart carrier' or less than a chief, takes the dead man to the women's island for burial. The women begin preparing the grave as soon as they see the boat coming. Quickly a huge feast is then put on, as part of a marriage ceremony, of sorts.

Malu is very serious about telling his story. But he doesn't realize he is switching languages in telling it.

Feleti asks him to continue telling the story in English, so the others can hear the story too.

Malu obliges, "Women have contest. Each woman already made chair. Chair made of whatever find on island. Each woman put chair on back. Man climb up on chair, on woman's back. Each woman take turn carrying man on back. Woman who carry man farthest, wins. Woman who carry farthest, get chance to carry child. Man stay on island 'til child born. If woman not have child by 330 settings of sun, then nother contest find nother woman for man."

Aleah tries not to let on how worried she is. She attempts to show interest, "So, the man returns to his island as soon as the child is born?"

Malu speaks directly to Aleah, "Soon as child born, nother contest. This time only boys. Boy who carry most buckets of water on pole, be *'chosen one'* of man. Boy then go with man back to man island."

Feleti laughs, "Best system of population control I've ever heard of."

Aleah does not laugh. She asks, "What you mean by *'chosen one'*? What 'chosen one' mean?" She catches herself speaking in the same broken English.

Malu looks into her eyes, "If I be *'chosen one'* of Feleti, when Feleti die, I bring him to woman island."

Aleah is thinking more in-depth about this than anyone else, "What if there is a weak boy who never wins a contest? Wouldn't the frailest boys become frail men and remain on the island?"

Malu begins talking at length in their native language. Feleti listens, taking great concern for what Malu is saying.

Aleah waits until Malu is done with his lengthy discourse, then addresses Feleti, "Is he aware that he switched back to his language again? What did he say just then?"

Feleti translates the unknown portion, "He said, no."

Aleah insists, "He said more than that!"

Feleti offers more, "Well, he said that when a boy is born, the mother nurses the boy until the boy can carry a pole with one full bucket of water on each end. When a girl is born, the mother nurses the girl until the girl can carry a boy on her back. This is the only training the children must go through. But now to answer your question, any boy who reaches the age of twelve, who has not won the bucket carrying contest, must leave the island, and promise never to return to either the men's or women's islands. Those 12-year-olds are considered weak, and usually become fisherman on some other island."

Aleah doesn't know why Malu has turned away, but trusts Feleti can perhaps still answer her question, "So, if there are a lot of girl babies born, and several years go by without anyone dying on the men's island—-then several strong boys soon to turn twelve could be banished because only one can win the contest. I know it's not my culture, nor am I the lawmaker of their way, but I'm just curious as to whether that could theoretically create a dilemma of sorts. Couldn't it diminish the number of available boys to potentially go to the men's island as a *'chosen one'*?"

Malu turns back around, "If girl born, man still return to man island. Then oldest *'chosen one'* on man island go to woman island. If girl born again, then next oldest *'chosen one'*. Next and next ...'til boy born."

Malu appears upset. He turns away again.

Aleah inquires, "What is wrong? Why does he keep turning away?"

Feleti explains, "Malu feels you are questioning things too much. Each of the islands have their own way of life. And they just accept things the way they are. Every country, every people, have their own culture, their customs, their traditions."

Aleah explains, "It's just that my daughter is lost out here somewhere and I'm a bit tense and concerned about what kind of people she may be running into. But we already know what kind of people live on these islands. People that we care about. That's why we are doing missionary work here. I thank Malu for refocusing my attention back to the reason we are all here. And I'll try hard not to let my emotions get in the way."

Feleti offers one last bit of knowledge, "You have to learn the ways of the islands if you want to leave a good impression."

Aleah adds, "I want to show them the ways of God ...not just leave a good impression. But, I see what you're saying."

Lorvin and Aleah take a private moment by themselves to pray, shedding more tears with their prayers.

Murray and Sweeney, on the other hand, find much interest in this cultural diversity. They listen as Feleti becomes an open history book to them, "Indonesia consists of between thirteen thousand and eighteen thousand islands, six thousand of which were for a long time uninhabited. But things changed at the beginning of the century, or millennium, as you would say. And some would say, organized crime began its influx in a big way at this time. We would prefer to say—-organized labor, which in and of itself is a crime. Big business was the reason they terrorized our people and set up labor camps, putting even our young children to work, under the cruelest of conditions. That's when some of the people felt they had no choice but to move about, and even inhabited some islands previously known to be uninhabited."

While Murray is most fascinated by the description of these people and their beliefs, Sweeney has one main focus, "What about Komodo dragons?" He had heard mention of Komodo Island. He assumes it was named after the reptilian wonder.

Feleti continues his history lesson, "No people used to live on Komodo Island, but in the 1800s the King of Indonesia sent criminals to Komodo Island to punish them. Their descendents continued to live there. Then in 1980, the entire island was declared a National Park and the Komodo dragons were protected. That same decade, a large fire on Padar Island destroyed many Komodo dragons, and the surviving Komodos swam to neighboring islands. This greatly dwindled their numbers and also their habitation. But surprisingly this same thing happened a couple decades later on

Komodo Island. Terrorists were responsible for destroying the National Park."

This peaks both Murray's and Sweeney's interest, as Feleti continues, "But worse, they terrorized our mission effort. We were doing great work, especially with the Weyewa, Sumbanese, and Tanimbarese people. The terrorists destroyed our missionary establishments. We had to relocate in 2015, to another island. We had to rebuild our headquarters and our whole strategy. Some of the islands that we felt had great promise, fell back to their old beliefs. Some even regressed so far that we have been unable to reach them."

Sweeney is upbeat, "It can't be all that bad, can it? We all have to rid ourselves of old beliefs sometime or another throughout our lives."

Feleti is a bit more serious, "Well, nothing's impossible, but it is often unsuccessful. These people were also told that a great evil was coming to their island. They didn't know when, but they were told to heed the warning. And they were warned that the 'great evil' would come if they heard the name of Jesus. They were told to guard themselves against any mention of Jesus. They were told they should do whatever is necessary ...to flee from any sort of evil and rid themselves of those who would come with such a troublesome message."

Murray inquires, "They made the name of Jesus ...as a curse?"

Sweeney confesses, "I honestly must admit that in a manner of speaking, which I should have in no way spoken, I did the same thing. My own country makes cursing commonplace, yet not out of fear, but rather of no account. Sadly, few so-called civilized people guard themselves against the misuse of the name of Jesus."

Lorvin continues to stand, staring across the waters. The island is still a good distance away, but it is coming into view. Malu joins Lorvin, but does not share in Lorvin's silence. Malu speaks the language in a rather choppy style, but he can be understood. He talks and talks ...and talks. But Lorvin isn't listening.

XXXI.

Moriah and Shannon had listened very carefully to Hola. But what choice did they have? Hola has them lost. They are uncertain whether it's intentional or not ...whether Hola is lost also. But at this point it is rather irrelevant. What is relevant though, is the fact that Hola appears to be less confident than he had been.

Yes, Hola appears to be somewhat fearful himself. The only advantage appears to be that there is a feast of some sort going on. It appears not to be a celebration feast, but rather a feast of atonement. If there is one thing that Hola does know for sure, it is about eating. And he is very confident that he knows the difference between one feast and another.

They had arrived at the island before sunrise. There'd been no sign of life on the island—-until the earth shook. Then there was a great awakening, of much activity. They suddenly focused on gathering up foods and other specific items—-with what appeared to be prompt preparations for some offering, to atone for their wrongdoings—-the apparent connection with the great quaking of the earth.

Hola had said that they might as well witness to the people as long as they are here. But what Moriah and Shannon are witnessing is perhaps a change of heart by Hola—-as they witness this great scurrying about of people.

Shannon is certain they would otherwise be seen—-if not for the intense focus of gathering together for what appears to be preparations for a feast. The people are simply too distracted in their panicked state. And Shannon is very glad for the distraction.

At this time, a huge parade or caravan formation is quickly assembled. At the head of the parade is what Hola calls a sedan chair. Four people carry it on two long poles. The poles support a chair surrounded by curtains. Only once do they get a glimpse of a person behind the curtains, as the pole carriers pass too closely to a tree branch, catching the curtain and temporarily pulling it back. The parade proceeds along a ridge, the sedan chair with pole carriers in front, followed by the long line of those serving a purpose similar to pack mules ...hunched over under the weight of their load of collected food substances.

Hola finds a path within the thicket below, following along the ridge above. Curiosity moves him, yet fear keeps him concealed within the path below. This path below is not a very frequently followed path, mostly overgrown with brush ...yet Hola quickly moves on, Shannon and Moriah with no option but to follow.

Hola leads, careful not to allow the snapping of a branch to be heard, and sure not to allow one to snap back in the faces of Moriah and Shannon who follow closely on his heels.

Twice Shannon's hair snags on the thicket. It not only hurts, but the snapping of a twig draws Hola's attention as he looks back. She quickly tucks her hair under her baseball cap.

Hola attempts to keep pace with the sedan chair. He moves with ease through the bush. Moriah and Shannon are not so accustomed to this. They manage to keep up, but don't know how much longer they'll be able to.

Suddenly the earth shakes again. Instinctively, they all freeze in their tracks. Hola, Moriah, and Shannon look up. Hola reacts quickly, stepping aside as a huge rock occupies the spot he once did.

One of the men carrying the pole of the sedan chair is too close to the edge of the ridge. He stumbles as another rock breaks loose. He slides over the edge of the ridge—-desperately grasping for anything. He manages to grip a small shrub—-also attempting to hang-on to the rocky soil.

This all brings on a chain of events of earthshaking proportion. The unbalanced weight at the front of the sedan chair, created by the missing pole carrier, causes the other lead pole carrier to trip.

The front drops, causing the poles to slide across the rocky path. The two rear pole carriers lower their end, attempting to level the ride ...but one pole slides over the ridge's edge. The lead pole carrier who had tripped, tries to regain his position, lifting up on his side ...which completely tips the sedan chair over.

Then the worst happens! Everyone on top of the ridge looks down, now discovering Hola, Moriah, and Shannon—-as their Chief tumbles out of the sedan chair and down the ridge, still caught within the curtains. And the Chief's frightening descent lands him right at Shannon's feet.

Shannon instinctively kneels beside him, moved by fear of the possible fatality of the event. Blood is streaked across the Chief's face, and matted throughout his long hair and beard.

While Shannon focuses her attention on the condition of the Chief, panic sets in for Hola and Moriah as they witness the natives quickly descending the ridge to their fallen leader. The imminent danger poses an uncertain outcome—-especially for Shannon, as they encircle her.

Shannon's eyes are shut, as she prays the Chief's fall not be fatal. She is not even aware that the tribal men have now gathered around her. Hola and Moriah stand speechless, powerless to do anything, except to also pray ...but with eyes as wide open as can be.

****

A much smaller procession, of seven, stroll along the water's edge. Feleti hadn't shared his fears with the others. He had feared how they'd get close to the island. Now that they are on the island, the others stand in fear of the sudden earthquake. But, Feleti doesn't fear the quake ...he fears the quaking spirit of Malu that is evident to him, and that he seems to be holding something back.

Feleti's interest is in using Malu's familiarity with the islands to aid them in befriending the islanders. He takes Malu to the side to talk privately. He wants to ask Malu how he knows so much about these islands. If the islanders fear anyone getting near, in fear that any visitor may be the evil one, then how did Malu get near enough to learn all these things?

Malu had not intended it this way, but says he will be of no help to Feleti or the others. He admits to having a great personal fear of the islanders. But an even greater fear is that the others will find out why.

Feleti wants to know what it is that Malu is not telling him. If they're to successfully work together to find Hola, Moriah, and Shannon, then they can't afford keeping any secrets—-as it may jeopardize their chance of a successful rescue effort.

Malu has one request, "You first agree not tell anyone."

Feleti honors that request, "Okay, I won't tell anyone. But you must tell me."

Malu lowers his voice. Though no one is in earshot, he still whispers, "Years ago, I ...one of twelve-year-olds, banished because of weakness."

As they now stroll down the sandy beach, Feleti presents his suggestion to Murray and Sweeney, "You know, we may have to give up Shannon's gift to gain their favor."

Murray has second thoughts, "Maybe I should have stayed with the ship. What if it isn't a friendly tribe?"

Feleti needs all the support he can get, and feels the heavy burden of response, "I don't really know. We missionaries have to face the fact that there's much we don't know, and we have to believe enough in what we are doing to take that chance."

Sweeney has a different perspective than his brother, "I'd rather take a chance with the natives here than to have to face Rebekkah if we don't find Shannon and deliver her the gift."

Suddenly, a group of natives come out of the thicket. The seven stand closely together as the natives walk within just a few feet of them—-holding sticks, clubs, and spears.

Murray whispers, "They don't look too friendly!"

Natives come out of the thicket at three more spots—-one furiously intimidating group closing in from behind and two other overeager groups approaching on each remaining side.

Sweeney reconsiders, "I think Rebekkah would understand." He turns to Feleti, "I think we should offer Shannon's gift to their Chief. I would so much like to make peace with these wonderful people. Feleti, please tell me you can make them happy!"

Feleti hesitates, "I think I understand part of what they are saying, but each island is slightly different. I'd rather not consider the possibilities of what might happen if I say something wrong. Give me a little extra time to think about this."

Murray can't contain himself, "We might not have a little extra time. Malu, you like to shoot the breeze—-say something. Say anything! You're from around these parts, tell them this is a gift for their Chief."

Feleti nods his approval, and whispers to Malu, "Malu ...you must say something! You were a child when you left ...they won't recognize you."

Malu has fear in his eyes, "How I explain how I know how to speak language so well."

Feleti is becoming impatient, "You think too much ...now start talking!"

Malu isn't quite sure, "Okay, but what if never seen before? Maybe afraid of what you call ...horse. Could be reason for spears and clubs. But, you the boss!"

Malu talks so fast that it would be difficult to believe anyone could understand even a word he says. And he says so much that they are wondering what all he's saying. Maybe it wasn't such a good idea to ask Malu to talk.

The circle suddenly widens, as the natives take a couple steps back. One native speaks what appears to be only five or six words.

Feleti, Kakau, Murray, Sweeney, Lorvin, and Aleah all look at Malu. But it is Lorvin who seems most eager to know, "Did you ask them if they've had any other recent visitors to the island?"

Malu is either a man of many words, or of few words, "No."

Feleti clarifies, "Malu told them we are friendly, that we mean no harm, and that we brought this gift for their Chief."

Lorvin doesn't understand, "Why are we giving them a gift? We are not certain whether Moriah and Shannon are even here."

Feleti asserts himself, as he has over the years in leadership, "We can't guarantee *we* will be here! When things get rough, we work with what we got. Besides, we can't go back on it now—-they've accepted our offer at this point. That one man said he'd get the Chief."

Several minutes go by. It seems like forever, but then the natives line up in two rows beside the thicket. Quickly out of the thicket emerges a makeshift stretcher between two poles. The four men are carrying what appears to be a human body.

They step to the side, and set the body down. It's impossible to tell whether the body is alive or not—-or for how long, in either state. It is also impossible to predict whether the same outcome will befall them ...as did the one left lying on the stretcher.

Then out of the thicket emerges a sedan chair adorned with curtains, and carried by four men between two poles. The one native who said he'd get the Chief, takes the gift from Sweeney.

Sweeney hesitates to give it over, but Feleti is the one calling the shots, so he lets go.

Suddenly Shannon leaps from behind the curtain of the sedan chair. Hola steps out next, and says something to Shannon—-to which she bursts with joy and wonderment, grabbing the reins of the Arabian horse, not yet seeing the newly arrived seven.

Moriah holds back the curtain. From her look-out she's not only seen above the rest, but also has a great vantage point. She views this ride more like that of an emperor's palanquin.

Upon seeing their daughter above the crowd, Lorvin and Aleah now race between the two rows of natives towards her. But Moriah is busy praying for their rescue while gazing out to sea, and doesn't immediately see them as they stride past Shannon and the horse.

Suddenly she sees who it is ...and leaps from the sedan chair and into her Daddy's open arms. The hug then extends itself to Aleah—-whose tears of joy and gratitude stream down her face.

Hola expects he'll be scolded severely by his brother—-who instead hugs him, saying nothing, the hug speaking for itself.

Shannon greets everyone with tears of joy, then attention is drawn to the most immediate concern. The man on the stretcher is in critical condition. He is in need of immediate care.

The ship has some medical supplies, but it's best he be treated at the hospital on the mission base island. Aleah is a well-trained nurse, and takes charge in that respect. She joins Murray and Sweeney in taking the injured man to the ship. Kakau also goes with them to help navigate back, and in case they need a translator along the way.

Feleti, Hola, Lorvin, Moriah, Shannon, and Malu all agree to stay on the island to carry out what already appeared to be in motion—-to bring God's Word and the message of Jesus to this island people. Murray and Sweeney pledge to return with supplies.

The natives look on with much interest as their visitors wave after saying goodbye and parting company. Even the natives pick up on it. They begin waving to the boat as it takes their old chief to the ship. They then turn, and begin waving to each other.

Some of the islanders continue to wave, but most of them turn their attention to Shannon as she rides up and down the beach at the water's edge on her Arabian horse. And she waves too.

The warm breeze catches a wisp of her hair, gently brushing it away from her face. Shannon smiles, embracing the full moment. She will name her horse—-Breeze.

Malu agrees that it is a good name, though he pronounces it ...*Bees*. But the rest of the crew agree they are more interested in other things ...like finding out how Shannon came about being named their new *'Chief'*.

Shannon isn't quite sure herself. But Malu is sure to find out. He has somehow overcome his fears, and he is talking up a storm with the islanders. It appears certain he will come up with the answer.

****

That evening, they gather together to come up with a plan—-a plan to present to these people—-the plan of salvation.

What Malu had shared with them would aid them in their plan. Malu had found out from the islanders how Shannon had become 'Chief'. Apparently, when the Chief's time to die came, it was customary that whoever was closest when he could no longer stand ...would become the new Chief. Apparently, the Chief was sick and was trying to let on that he wasn't. But they all knew that he was ...and were letting on too. They had planned the longer route to the mountain plateau because it was more rocky. They had hopes that the rocky ride would make the Chief sicker.

The pole bearers had been hopeful the Chief would fall out of the sedan chair at one of their feet. But as it was, the Chief fell down the ridge and landed at Shannon's feet. And as they had gathered around her, their pathway was clear. They had no choice, but to bow to Shannon ...as their new Chief.

The islanders did not necessarily respect their custom, but they appeared to fear opposing it. That was a form of respect. They'd perhaps wished it another way, but they had no other choice. If they departed from their own customs, they'd be departing from that which they all accepted. And new ideas may bring forth difference of opinion, then eventually the threat of division and lawlessness. That is what they had fled from, and no one seemed to want to risk returning to that.

The pole bearers had admitted this to Malu—-which was a good sign. Confession of wrongdoing is an integral part in the salvation message. This seems to hold true for most cultures. If they are open to admitting they've been tempted to oppose their own rules, then they've indicated they understand the importance of doing what is right. Then if they're told their right is actually wrong, they can continue on with learning to understand what is truly right.

Feleti cautions the group. They will follow the New Tribes approach of teaching, but they will hold off longer in mentioning the name of Jesus. The terrorist groups had taught to guard against anyone who would mention Jesus—-and this island group had probably heeded the warning, even though it appears they had possibly fled the main areas where terrorist activity had gotten a foothold, establishing its strongholds.

There is hope. The rumor is that this island group and culture had only established itself a little more than a couple generations ago. It is believed that these two islands—-this one which the men occupy and the other one which the women occupy—-had been previously uninhabited by humans. But that all had changed when the terrorists destroyed Komodo Island. The natives and the Komodos had both left for ...apparently these two islands.

Malu does not like Komodo dragons—-no one he knows does, but his fear of them is way beyond most—-based on a childhood fear. There is no present evidence of Komodo dragons, but he is certain to ask, "Wh-wh-a-whe-r-e, where are Komodos?"

He suddenly realizes it, and has to repeat the question in their language.

They inform Malu that the Komodos are confined to the South half of the men's island. The women had successfully herded them off their island by using fire, and those Komodos also swam to the South half of the men's island ...where they reportedly flourished. No doubt, the islanders fed them so well! Malu also is told that the Komodos are considered the guardians of the mountain, the guardians of the *'Man in the mountain'*.

The men's island is divided in two by a deep canyon. The older men remember when the two halves of the island had split in the mountains. It would've divided further, but the Chief returned the *'Man in the mountain'* to his rightful place in the mountain, and peace was restored.

Feleti suggests to the missionary group that they not attempt to discourage them from their native practice of taking food to the mountains. "Our goal is not to offend their beliefs. In time, they will replace their beliefs with the truth."

Feleti tells Hola that he can lead the teaching, since he came here for that sole purpose. Feleti anticipates the teaching may go smoother than in many other areas. The language of this island is not that much different. And Malu can aid him greatly in any translation barriers, since he appears to understand significantly more than anyone else. Feleti does not tell why. He will respect Malu's request that no one find out why.

So, it is settled. As their new Chief, Shannon will direct the islanders to listen and learn. They will watch Hola teach, and listen to Malu translate. At Shannon's direction, they will hear, and learn the message of salvation.

Meanwhile, they will join the islanders as they continue to feed the Komodos—-which they refer to as *'guardians of the mountain'*. And they will also continue to prepare food for the *'Man in the mountain'*, who they obviously believe is a deity.

Feleti stresses his point over and over, "We should not set out to offend their belief system, but to guide them in truth. That will allow them to choose their own readiness to replace each of their beliefs with the truth."

The others agree. Establish mutual respect first. That will aid in a greater depth of attentiveness, and a commitment to learning.

As Shannon joins them at the mountain plateau to feed the Komodos, she makes her announcement, "This will be the area we will do the teaching."

Malu wishes this would have been one of the things discussed in advance. He whispers to Feleti, "Have to teach in area where Komodos are?"

Feleti whispers back his response, "Announce it to the people as she has requested. In order to dispel their superstitions, we must stand courageous before their fears. We must together witness the emptiness of their demigods and their deities. And you must understand the great opportunity this provides to bond with their people, without caving-in to their beliefs."

****

Shannon directs them to take the shortcut, not the rocky ridge. And she chooses not to ride in the sedan chair. "No more sedan chair ...no wait!"

Malu is about to translate that, but Shannon changes her mind. She will keep the sedan chair, but she will not ride in it. The Bible and the teaching materials will occupy that sacred and respected place behind the curtains.

Shannon chooses instead to ride her horse. It is a rather easy ride from the northwest corner of the island, instead of the rocky route along the ridge at the northeast. It's an easy and enjoyable ride through the foothills. But then the elevation changes more significantly. There are challenging spots, yet not unmanageable for Breeze.

It is difficult to appear humble—-riding aloft and not to appear aloof, as she lets her horse gallop ahead at times. Any horse would amaze a people who had never seen a horse before. But Shannon had seen and read about enough horses to know this one stands above the rest. This black Arabian is a combination of strength and beauty—-with its muscular lines and unchallenging confidence. Her horse ascends the mountain like it is nothing—-it's simply a 'breeze'.

Lorvin is a student of geology—-from a Christian perspective. The land being the teacher—-and of course, the Bible. Lorvin judges this island to be very unstable. By the looks of the land, there had been much volcanic and earthquake activity which brought the island to its present condition.

At its highest point, the ridge juts out, creating the narrowest point of the canyon. Breeze stops under a large tree, gracing the point, a plateau stretching out on the other side of the canyon, only fifty feet away at this point.

When the others finally reach their destination, they join Shannon for the breath-taking view. It is also a great vantage point. You can see the entire island from here, and anyone who may be approaching the island by sea. No one should be able to approach the island without detection. And the women's island can just barely be seen from here also. Malu points it out, as the islanders point it out to him.

* * * * * * * *

The islanders call to the *guardians of the mountain*.

They take their turns at the point. A rope is tied to the handle of each large basket, and the other end tied around their waist. The natives begin to twirl the huge basket of food below their waist. They begin twirling low and extend the circle to over their head. Then they release the basket from their hand like the 'hammer throw' of track and field events ...except for the rope part. If they don't release it just right, the food won't leave the basket, and the weight of it may propel them into the canyon as extra Komodo treats.

Malu steps back. Even from his safe distance, he doesn't want to see the Komodos, as they come for their food. The others step forward to see if they can see the Komodos. But they step back again as the fourth person begins twirling his basket. This time the rope is released, basket and all clearing the canyon.

The missionary group is confused as they watch the fifth, sixth, and seventh baskets clear the canyon and land on the plateau. Then to their surprise, natives run out from behind some rocks, and begin devouring the baskets of food that had landed on the plateau.

Malu quickly tries to clear up any possible misunderstandings. Apparently, there are various levels of *guardians of the mountain*. The Komodos are one level ...and these natives, seemingly trapped on the plateau and eager for food, are another level of *guardians*.

At this point, the question curiously becomes, whether the *Man in the mountain* is actually, *Men in the mountain*. But Malu quickly asks and clears that one up too. There is only one *'Man in the mountain'*.

Feleti assumes that the sole *'Man in the mountain'* is a chief of sorts. Shannon is the Chief of the lowlands and they probably had a designated *'Man'* of the mountains.

Shannon observes for a moment as the natives devour the food on the plateau. But she is more interested in the Komodos. She had never seen a Komodo dragon before. She grabs a tree branch to steady herself near the edge of the cliff, peering down into the canyon. She does not look long though. It is not a pretty sight. She can understand Malu's feelings about it.

Shannon steps back by Malu. She remembers that she had packed Cody Komodo. She takes Cody out of the small purse attached to her belt. She thinks of Leah. Her sister certainly wouldn't have had such kindly affection to Cody if she had first seen the real Komodos. Shannon thinks of Mom, Josiah, and Samuel too. She misses them all.

Shannon steps towards the empty baskets. She is overcome by such a foul smell.

Malu laughs at seeing her facial expression. He explains that the baskets hold two different types of food. Half of the baskets are prepared for the natives on the plateau. The other baskets, Malu very descriptively explains, "Komodo food. Gather all rotting carcasses can find along shore."

Shannon interrupts, "Okay, you can stop now. Or my lunch will have to be added to their menu."

Malu is prompted to ask his next question, "How islanders, guardians, get on plateau?"

The one man in charge of the food baskets, Siaosi, laughs. Then Siaosi speaks to the others—-and they laugh together. Siaosi then calls out several times, "Tevita, Tevita, Tevita."

A young man with the brightest smile and near perfect teeth, steps from the back of the group. Siaosi and the young man converse privately by the large tree, then the young man begins to climb the tree.

The young man, Tevita, climbs three-quarters of the way up the tree, then crawls out on a limb. He appears to have a rope in his hands. Suddenly, he springs from the branch like a frog off a log. The rope carries him swinging beyond the cliff, out over the canyon. At its furthest point, he lets go of the rope, does a backward flip through the air and lands on a heap of something.

Malu translates, "Dried grass."

The question then becomes—-how does the young man, Tevita, or any of the others get back if they choose to do so?

As Malu prepares to speak, the natives begin to laugh again.

Lorvin smiles, "Yes, it appears that smiles and laughter are a universal language, but what one laughs at can vary greatly. What are they laughing at this time?"

Malu translates, "Think funny how you think they not know how do things."

This time Siaosi climbs up the tree. He pulls the end of the rope back up with him and appears to be fastening it to something. With a large kick from one of his legs, a large timber moves out away from the tree trunk, falling straight towards the plateau.

Lorvin is amazed, "I'd have to see it again to see precisely how he did that."

Feleti joins the inspection, "Two timbers tied together with one end tied down at the base of this tree and the rope tied precisely at the right spot, with just the right firmness of slip-knot to guide the timber out, but not allowing the rope to break and not allowing the timbers to fall too hard onto the plateau. Seems easy, but I still could not do it and don't know how they did it."

Lorvin realizes the island people have engineering skills and athletic abilities that far exceed what anyone might expect. They are out of his league, yet Lorvin feels compelled to say something, "Two timbers tied together, so it doesn't roll, and I saw over a dozen slip-knots each timed just right ...simply amazing!"

Shannon doesn't say anything, though she too is amazed. She had seen people do some amazing stunts in gymnastics, and she had seen the expertise of tree trimmers back home in Michigan. But these natives, usually considered uncivilized, had obviously trained themselves in these skills.

Tevita walks confidently across the timbers, crossing back over the canyon. He retrieves the rope, walks about three-quarters of the way back out, ties the rope securely around the timbers, then returns to the tree. Tevita climbs the tree, joining Siaosi. Together, the two of them pull the rope back, retrieving the timbers to their original position against the tree.

Shannon has Malu ask them why the others voluntarily remain on the plateau?

Malu reports, "Because 'guardians of mountain' ....take care of 'Man in mountain'. All agree it most important of all."

Shannon shares her idea with Feleti, Lorvin, Moriah, and Hola, "I was going to teach on this side, under the shade of the tree, but now I want to have the teaching over there on the plateau. Shouldn't they hear the salvation message too?"

They all agree. But will the natives agree?

Shannon asks Malu to ask, "Am I the Chief of the guardians also?"

Malu translates back, "Yes."

Shannon smiles at Malu, "Well, tell them I want to teach them on that plateau over there. But tell them I want to cross on a bridge which is strong enough and wide enough for my horse to cross on. Ask them how long it will take to build such a bridge."

Malu shares Shannon's request with Siaosi and Tevita.

Siaosi smiles, saying something to Tevita. They each raise their right hands ...then they high-five each other.

Malu asks, then reports back, "Three days to build bridge. But for Chief Shannon—-two days. And bridge be strong as ten horses."

****

The bridge is done in two days, but Shannon waits until early on the third to lead the caravan of people, with more food, up the mountain.

Shannon dismounts her horse as they reach the point. She sends the sedan chair with the teaching materials over first. Then as soon as the sedan chair crosses the new bridge, safely over to the plateau, she leads her horse over. The others then follow.

Hola leads the teaching. Feleti keeps his word, stating that Hola had come to the island to teach, and teach he shall.

Feleti's only caution for them is to not mention the name of Jesus until the end, when they are fully prepared to accept it.

Hola uses Shannon and Moriah to assist him with the materials and the presentation. Malu still has the crucial part of translating what Hola is teaching, so they can understand.

Hola begins teaching about Adam and Eve. He describes the garden, sort of like an island on land. They are the only two in that garden. And God gives them everything they need ...but they want what God says isn't theirs to have.

Hola teaches the *'New Tribes Mission'* approach, with their guidelines of teaching the Bible in chronological order. And each time, Hola's words are translated by Malu.

They listen with much interest as Abraham and Isaac go up the mountain. And they are thankful for the provision of the ram in the thicket. They also feel Esau is not deserving of the blessing that Jacob receives. And they agree that Jacob's sons do not know how to get along. They feel sorry for Joseph when his brothers sell him into slavery. And they feel sorry for Jacob when he is told that his son is dead. They really like Joseph's character. They think it is really good how Joseph forgives his brothers.

The most significant impact though, begins with the teaching of Moses. Hola tells how Pharaoh orders for all male babies to be killed, but Moses is saved in a floating basket. Hola consults with his brother, Feleti, going over his intended strategy. The natives had already admitted how their hopes to become Chief had led them to take the long route up the mountain. Hola shows how God chooses who He wants, and puts that person in place to become the leader.

Then to everyone's surprise, Hola inadvertently changes his strategy, jumping to the end of the teaching plan. He suddenly tells them of all the baby boys 'Chief Herod' had killed while trying to kill the One who was God's own Son. But, before they get too carried away, he mentions that just like baby Moses was hidden ...God's Son was hidden too.

The fear moves across their faces. One of the natives, named Fangatua, is interpreted by Malu, "God's Son? Why God let His Son come here?"

Hola listens to the intensified whispering among the natives. He believes this is good. "Good question ...you ask why God's Son would sacrifice all the comforts of being God, and come to earth, not staying with His Father in heaven? Why would God's Son live within the burden of all that is wrong—-the bad shared by each of us who lives here? The answer is that God's Son was to live among them as their new leader."

Hola lets that sink in, yet for barely a moment, "And that is why Chief Herod was so upset. Chief Herod was not living the way he should be, and he was enjoying life in a way he should not be.

So Chief Herod didn't want a new leader to lead them in a much different way—-in the correct way. Chief Herod knew he was wrong the way he was living, but he didn't want anyone to spread the word that they could choose to follow a new leader."

At this, Fangatua speaks out loudly, with Malu's translation, "That's stupid! Why he think he get away with trying to kill God's Son? Chief Herod made God much angry. Did God make earth shake?"

Hola wants them to really want to hear the truth. He wants them to love the story, the way he loves these true life events, "God does not like killing, but God is not to be looked upon as always being angry. God loves us and wants us to live a good life. And when God's Son began to grow, old Chief Herod was no longer Chief, there was a new Chief. And God's Son was safe as a boy, sitting just like you are sitting. He listened and He obeyed. Then He became a man—-and He told people the truth of how to live. Some listened and believed, and they were no longer sad. But some listened and did not believe ...they didn't want to believe. Some people don't like to be told the truth, they just stay angry ...and they become friends with other angry people, even if they don't like them."

Fangatua is joined by others, also expressing emotions, as Malu interprets, "Why angry ...first place?"

Hola explains, "They didn't want to hear of God's Son healing the sick and causing the blind to see. They thought that a leader like that was too good. And it didn't do them any good. All they saw was people changing the way they lived. And they didn't want to change. They didn't want to hear anything about this new leader or this new way to live. They didn't look to what happiness others were gaining, but to what they'd lose. Getting rid of God's Son was the only way they felt their lives would remain peaceful. That is the way angry people get—-thinking the only way is to get rid of what is making them angry, not trying to change *themselves* into less angry people."

"They think they can get rid of God? That real stupid too ...only make God angry more. God shake 'em up ...God really shake the earth."

Hola raises his voice to emphasize the point, "They thought if they killed God's Son—-any memory of Him could be hidden and forgotten. So that's what they did ...they killed God's Son."

Fangatua's anger cannot be silenced, "Now I angry ...wish I been there to shake the rocks and mountain. I can tell God still angry 'bout it. God still shakin' the rocks."

Hola admits, "Well, God does get angry ...God gets angry when someone tries to take away from how He loves us. God's anger is towards people like Chief Herod who try to kill anyone who brings the truth. God's anger is also towards all the people who try to stop the hearing of the message of His truth. Each of those babies killed when God's Son was born, had they not been killed, could have later heard the message of truth. And each of them could have grown up ...to share it with others. God's anger is against anyone who tries to kill the truth."

A young man named, Mouk, speaks up with great concern. His words are translated back with equal emotion, "But not able to kill the truth. You bringing us truth today."

Hola feels the time is now right, "You are right. They couldn't kill the memory of Him. The truth could not be hidden. But they felt they could make the truth as if it were a lie. And they are still attempting to do that today. They would tell you that if you ever hear this—-that it is a lie."

Mouk seems to hold a burden he desperately wants to release. Others join him, repeating what he says. Malu relays the message of their conviction, "But when hear lies about God's Son, we not believe lies."

For the first time, Hola drops his head, looking away from them. Then he turns back, looking right at Mouk. Hola appears to look right through him, "You already have believed their lies about God's Son. You want to know, so I will tell you. The truth is that God's Son was given the name ...Jesus."

The group becomes very silent. Hola knows the people have been told not to listen to anyone who mentions the Name of Jesus.

Mouk approaches Malu, Feleti, and Hola. He looks into Hola's eyes, then Mouk begins to pace back and forth in front of them, mumbling to himself. He then looks over at Moriah and Shannon.

Suddenly, Mouk blurts out, interpreted by Malu with intense emotion, "Told of how all had hopes of becoming new Chief, but that not all. Our wrong thoughts grew. We welcomed sickness of Chief, we welcomed his death. But that not all. Also welcomed the death of ones appointed as guardians over us, own chosen ones—-because all burials are on women's island."

Hola listens intently. Malu had shared with them the belief that when the dead were buried, the woman—-chosen through her victory in the contest—-would spend her days near the gravesite, gaining a new life inside her, generated from out of the grave.

This whole discourse, like every other communication, has to be spoken in fragments repeated back from the island language to the language that the teachers can understand. Hola congratulates Malu, "It's amazing how much you've improved on your language. I wondered how this would work, but you are doing quite well."

The excitement builds as Mouk talks faster and the translator, Malu, also speaks faster, "That not all. One more thing—-some of us found plant, causing severe stomach pain, gave leaves of bad plant to woman—-so she lose child."

How horrible! The question *"why"* is on the mind of each of the teachers. They are not quick to recall the island traditions.

The answer refreshes their memory, "That way we stay longer on women's island. Had to stay 'til child born."

Tears gather in Mouk's eyes. It is difficult for him to speak. Tears also gather in Malu's eyes, as he interprets, "Mouk say he no better than Herod. He help kill babies. And same babies, if lived, been here today, hearing truth."

Upon hearing the very emotional confessions, Lorvin, Moriah, Shannon, Feleti, Malu—-and even Hola, characteristically very reserved, begin to shed tears—-joining Mouk's anguish over the bonds of sin.

The extent of the tribe's sin had been far from being realized. Sin has the tendency to heap upon itself—-which is the nature of unchecked sin. So instead of what we would think would be the natural inclination to confess it, actually does not lend itself towards that direction at all. Sin that is unconfessed, not only grows outwardly, but also tightens its grip within us—-on every little sin that enjoins its authority upon us. But confession changes the authority—-and can free us, with a quickness, from the tight grip which we could not free ourselves from. The young man, Mouk, could soon realize this, but there is one more thing that has to be taught before it can be experienced.

When it's realized, it can finally come out all at once. Yet, if someone proceeds their own way, it can be problematic. Better to abandon one's own way, and accept His way. God had already touched Mouk's heart because of his willingness to listen. At this moment, the confessions flow out of him. And it touches the hearts of many others—-and they also confess, recalling one thing after another.

For this small missionary team—-it means so much more. They know the breath of what is being opened up to these people. There is nothing greater that can be shared ...except what is to be shared next.

Even though the natives had begun to confess, they are yet to feel genuine forgiveness. But, Hola doesn't want to interrupt their confessions. They should be given whatever time they need to reach deep within themselves to identify the wrongs ...before things are made right.

* * * * * * * * *

Here on the islands, these natives had just acknowledged losing an unborn child—-no different than losing a child. To them it was unquestionably a child. There is no hiding the truth. They were there when the woman hemorrhaged—-pretending to comfort her, when in reality, they had caused it.

They had seen the graphic details. Nothing hid the fact that it was a real child. The only fact that was hidden ...was what caused the horrible death of the child, which the women cried for days over.

Mouk confesses that he understands the spirit of what caused Herod to put all those babies to death. It was the horrible sin of selfishness, and a stubborn unwillingness to change. And it is the same horrible spirit that brought the people to kill Jesus ...and it is the same spirit that's been living within him and the others.

Lorvin and Moriah hug each other. This is what they had learned in their brief mission training. It is an experience, unmatched by any other on earth. And it is just the beginning. Their own tears of joy and love for these people, now mix with the tears of renewed and increased levels of appreciation and gratitude for what God did in sending His Son ...what His Son did—-in dying on the cross.

As the natives continue to confess their horrible practices, the teachers do not let what they are hearing generate any feelings of anger against a people who some would feel should certainly be judged for the horrible things they've done. It is the wonderful thing that Jesus did—-dying on the cross, sacrificing His life so we can have the truth—-so we can be forgiven, and so we can be free. As Jesus said on the cross, "Forgive them Father, for they know not what they do."

They had not known the extent of what they had done ...but, they had known enough, and that's why they were now confessing it. There was so much wrong, and no feeling as to how to deal with the past ...but to repeat it, over and over again. They did not have a good view of themselves, so they'd just continued on. They needed those gentle words which Jesus spoke to the woman who was about to be stoned to death ..."Neither do I condemn you. Go, and sin no more!"

You can see the sincerity of the natives. There is no debate whether what they did was wrong, or not. It is quite certain they will stop their horrible practices. All they have to be told now is the truth of Jesus' death on the cross as a sacrifice for their sins. And by grasping onto that truth, holding onto the awesome love that grants us forgiveness through Jesus, they can be assured they are forgiven. Then, and only then can they experience the joys of living the way God wants for them ...through accepting Jesus.

At this moment, Hola shares with them that Jesus came back to life ...and that Jesus forgives them, if they will only allow Him to lead, to be truly 'chief' among them.

They suddenly become quiet, and they look back and forth at each other with an expression of desperation and hurt. Then the expression changes as one by one the realization hits each of them. They begin hugging each other, and then group hugs which bring them to dancing up and down in a circle. The circle grows into a huge group hug. They no longer fear that God will destroy them for what they've done. God wants to *lead* them because He *loves* them ...and He forgives them.

They now believe, and the torment is gone. The freeing of the burden of guilt and sin becomes so real, there is no experience that comes close to describing it. They continue to jump for joy ...and their spontaneous victory dance celebrates the freeing moment they've found through Jesus' conquering sin and death.

Shannon, Moriah, and Lorvin share a big hug with each other. Why is this so difficult for their own country to grasp? The most advanced nation on earth, bursting with knowledge, yet not bursting with the joy of Jesus. So simple—-that the most advanced cannot grasp it?

Feleti smiles, "Just out of curiosity, brother—-and by the way, you did an excellent job. I'm just a bit curious. You really surprised us when you suddenly skipped a whole bunch of teaching, jumping from Moses straight to Jesus."

Hola smiles with an even bigger smile, "Thanks for the kind words, brother. I didn't think I was going to do that either, but 'fishers of men' must also know precisely the moment to pull in the catch. I suddenly felt it, and didn't want to lose them."

Something is still bothering Shannon. She can definitely grasp all the truth. She had cried in sorrow when the islanders had confessed about the unborn babies. She had cried intensely then. She had tears each time there was a vivid description of how Jesus died on the cross for us. But there are no tears now. She wants the tears to come—-she begins to cry because the tears won't come. Then more tears come through mere frustration. Like the others, Shannon's face is ridden with tears, but not the same kind of tears. The others have tears of joy for one another—-hers are tears of frustration, locked up within herself.

Shannon gets a glimmer of understanding. Maybe that's why she had judged Stan for not crying—-because of her own problem. Poor Stan had a much worse childhood than most had to endure. He probably had the same kind of emotions locked inside. But that did not take away anything from Stan. The good feelings were still there—-coming out in the most wonderful way. He is gentle, sensitive, and caring—-he just doesn't cry. But his lack of tears never seems to affect his wonderful sensitivity. Stan will certainly make Leah happy ...and Shannon is happy for her sister.

Shannon feels her oversensitivity sometimes gets in the way, blocking her sensitivity. And she feels guilty because she is crying for herself, not in joy for the others.

She had been disappointed with her first trip out here to the mission field. Now, this second time she thought it would be different—-and it is. Just not the way she wants.

She had seen how God used her for His purpose. She was a vital part of God's plan—-becoming Chief, as the first step in leading the islanders. But that was all God's doing. She had done nothing herself. She still feels she is missing what the others have. She wants the joy. She wants the inner-driven purpose and focus—-and the intensity of it.

Shannon feels guilt again. She should be satisfied with just being used by God, but she wants to do *her thing*—-maybe not so much even her thing, but—-her part. She definitely had a big part in all of this, at least at the start. But now she feels isolated from the rest ...lacking in the joy of celebration.

That must have been how Hola had felt. It was wrong what Hola had done—-extremely wrong. The end does *not* justify the means. But even Hola realizes he is justified in another sense—-justified through Christ, his Lord, Jesus. And Hola has found the joy. Through this island adventure, he has found the joy Shannon is still looking to experience.

Shannon has held back her emotions her whole life. She doesn't really trust her emotions. What would it take? She trusts God—-so why not just act on what she knows is right—-and let the emotions fall into place afterwards?

Shannon pictures in her mind—-the job of a firefighter. They put all fear aside, and just act like they know they have to. And when they save a life, no one questions whether they are crying or not. Most of the time we don't know the person who performs the heroics. And the one who is saved seldom knows the person who saves them—-but they are grateful. The firefighters seldom sit at the person's table to eat, nor are they invited over for holidays—-but instead, they go back out to risk their lives in saving others. And it is doubtful that they sit around talking about the lives they save, any more than they'd talk about the lives lost. They just do their job. It's too scary, too painful, and much too unproductive to sit around and dwell on it. When their moment comes, they know it's their moment. And they respond, without hesitation ...risking their lives.

Shannon doubts it will ever become her moment. And even now, just thinking about it—-it appears prideful—-wanting to be a hero. No true firefighter would hope for there to be a fire, so they could perform heroics. They'd rather there never be any fires. They'd prefer there be no lives to save. But as Shannon sees it, everyone needs to be saved—-saved from eternal death. And we need to accept Jesus' ready and awaiting rescue.

There is nothing in life of more significance. But as the islanders jump up and down for joy, Shannon still feels it is not her joy. She wants to tell herself differently, but she has to be honest with herself—-she doesn't feel like she is a part of all this.

XXXII.

The islanders are so busy with their eyes upon Jesus, they don't keep a vigilant watch out to sea. But it doesn't matter. They can see a new direction. And they are eager to visit the women's island—-to share the truth with them.

Shannon rides ahead, but not too far, as they parade down the mountain trail in joyful dance. As the path breaks to the open beach, a surprise awaits them. Murray and Sweeney have returned. With their celebratory festivities, they hadn't even seen them coming.

The bigger surprise awaits Moriah. Mom is eager to give her a big hug. But she is not the only one eager to see her. Lorvin's two sisters and his brother join the happy hugging party.

As they all hug and begin to tell their stories, Shannon focuses on that which comes a bit natural to her—-that which carries burdens and sorrow. She approaches Sweeney, "How is the old Chief doing?"

Shannon had witnessed how God had worked salvation to this island people—-through the passing on of the chieftain status. But Shannon is not primarily concerned with the status. Her concern is more for the person—-and her prayer is that he has not passed on.

Sweeney doesn't know what is going on, but he can at least sense that something more is going on with Shannon, "The old Chief was not doing well when I left him. The mission hospital is a good hospital, but they can *not* do miracles ...they can only pray for one. Old Chief has the island sickness, as some call it. They are not sure what brings it on, but only one in a hundred make it through."

Malu passes the message on. Many of the islanders had thought they'd witnessed their old Chief die. But they are happy to hear he hasn't died, and that he has a chance to live. The islanders ask Malu to help them pray for their old Chief.

Shannon and the others are very touched by the immediate concern of the islanders. They join hands with the islanders, and lead them in their first prayer.

Later that evening, Shannon inquires more about the island sickness, "Is it contagious?"

Lorvin is very familiar with the sickness, "Very much so. The islanders call it, white man's sickness. The islanders never get it. But it has wiped out more than a few of our missions. They used to call it missionary dysentery because of the initial symptoms, but they've found this variation to be tragically different ...though many still refer to it as missionary dysentery."

* * * * * * *

The next morning, plans are being made for the missionary group to depart. Shannon is grooming her beloved horse when one of the islanders, Uata, approaches with a crudely built wooden box.

Malu steps between Uata and Shannon. From the tone of each of their voices and the expressions on their faces, you can tell this is serious talk.

Malu had been told that Uata was the oldest of their tribe. He also was the most resistant to change. Not all the islanders readily accepted the salvation message. There is a small group, led by Uata, who had heard the message, but are hesitant to accept it. Uata likes the old traditions. He is an old warrior. And he is known to fight for what he believes in.

There is quite an intense exchange of words, then Malu steps aside.

Uata steps forward, and hands Shannon the wooden box.

Malu explains, "Uata say this Old Chief's box. Box supposed to pass on new Chief, but Uata say he know you not believe in sacred box. Uata say you give box to Old Chief—-maybe it help him feel better. Maybe box help heal him, and he can become Chief again."

Shannon needs encouragement at this time, not this. She not only feels she isn't a part of the joy that most of the islanders are feeling, now she is associated with this recently revealed division of thought. They are looking for answers, but she can't just jump right in and provide what they were looking for. She has too many questions herself. She can't rise to this occasion either. It definitely is not her moment!

Shannon turns to Hola, who is standing nearby, "Why are some of the people still burdened? What did we fail to teach them?"

Hola puts a comforting hand on Shannon's shoulder as he stands beside her, "Uata is the keeper of sacred things. The box he has just given you contains some things, Malu has told me, which are very much the foundation of what they believe. They want to believe all we have taught them, but they are not ready to walk away from all the things they have believed in. Abandoning all their old beliefs, to some of them, would be equivalent to denying their own sanity."

Shannon is confused, "What do you mean, denying their own sanity?"

Hola points to Uata, kneeling on the ground, facing away from them. It appears to Shannon that Uata is praying. Hola steps in front of Shannon, "I've been wanting to look inside this box."

Shannon steps back, "Now that would be insane! If they believe so strongly that this is a sacred box, why would I chance letting you open it?"

Shannon has many questions, "I still don't understand how abandoning their old beliefs would be challenging their sanity. We've taught them so much to help lighten their burden ...while keeping the old beliefs must be a daily struggle. You heard their confessions. They knew they were doing wrong. If I tried to live in denial—-that would challenge my sanity."

Hola steps back, assuring Shannon that he won't touch the box, "Now, answer me this—-would a sane person believe there is a *'Man in the mountain'*?"

Shannon attempts to choose her words carefully, "I get what you are saying. There are many beliefs that people have that they don't know are wrong. Like the *'Man in the mountain'*. Sometimes it takes a while to replace the old beliefs with the new. But I like the way you handled the teaching. Once you began teaching the truth about God, the *'Man in the mountain'* never made an appearance. I would say that made a rather convincing statement in itself."

Hola appears to summarize the thinking, "So, you do know why the *'Man in the mountain'* appeared to take a leave of absence?"

Shannon also summarizes, "The old beliefs were replaced by the truth, and the truth is ...there is no *'Man in the mountain'*."

Hola looks over at Uata, who is still kneeling on the sand, "Perhaps some believe that the *'Man in the mountain'* was sick. You know, the entire time I was teaching, we never fed him."

Shannon is confused, "Is that what they told you?"

Hola looks into Shannon's eyes, "Malu tells me that Uata has shown him."

Shannon is surprised with what Hola is saying. She thought Malu believed the same as they did. "Uata has shown Malu what?"

Hola is serious, "Malu has seen pictures of the *'Man in the mountain'*. Uata told Malu that the *'Man in the mountain'* had tried to escape, but Old Chief caught him, and had him sent back to the mountain."

Shannon suddenly realizes, "Oh, pictures—-you mean, things like rock carvings and drawings?"

Hola is very direct, "No, I mean—-photographs! Inside the sacred box. Malu said he saw photographs of the *'Man in the mountain'*. Now I know there is no man-God living in the mountain, but I'm saying that it seems there is a man up there that they believe is a friend of God. He had apparently tried to escape, but the Old Chief returned him so God wouldn't get angry. They say that ever since they had returned God's friend, the mountain has not shook—-until just before we came to the island."

A horrible thought comes to mind. Shannon had heard of how certain tribes had treated missionaries who had tried to bring them the Gospel of Jesus. Some tribes had gone so far, they sacrificed missionary persons in a volcano. She has a bad feeling about this. Perhaps a missionary person had come to the island. Perhaps he had referred to himself as a 'friend of God'.

Shannon doesn't want to consider this horrible thought any further, but the thought feeds itself. What if they had sent the missionary to the mountain, waiting for the mountain to take him?

The mountain had shown some recent instability. That was perhaps in Shannon's favor, choosing the mountain plateau as the location to teach, showing no fear. But as the tribe's fears seem to have been calmed, she is not at all calm. Fear now grips her. It sounds like there is a fellow missionary up in that mountain. And what if 'Old Chief' had condemned him, and sent him to a place surrounded by canyons teeming with Komodo dragons? Likely it would be a place he couldn't escape from ...and perhaps could it be the very place where they had just shared the Gospel?

Could their teaching have been responsible for the man's death? He could have been injured and in need of care, but they had felt no need to concern themselves with false beliefs about a *'Man in the mountain'*. They had stopped feeding him. And this was all under the direction of Shannon. After all, she was the new Chief.

Suddenly, Shannon wants to open the sacred box too. But Uata had asked her to give it to the Old Chief. She doesn't want to offend him. She holds the sacred box in her hands. Uata is still kneeling on the sand, facing away from her.

Slowly and cautiously, Shannon approaches Uata. She doesn't want to disturb him if he's praying.

Hola and Malu are at Shannon's side as she moves slowly around in front of Uata. Shannon is surprised to see that Uata is not praying. He has a deck of playing cards spread out on the sand in front of him.

Shannon doesn't say anything—-perhaps this is a strange sort of ritual, and she doesn't want to disturb him. The old tattered playing cards could be further evidence that a missionary had come to the island. But even that would seem odd. Why would the missionary even have a deck of cards? You'd think they'd have plenty to do. You'd think they would never be so bored that they'd resort to playing—-Solitaire? Uata is playing Solitaire!

Suddenly, the earth shakes! It startles Shannon. And she drops the sacred box on the ground, right in front of Uata. She doesn't want to offend Uata's sacred traditions. But she has just dropped the sacred box. What should she do?

Shannon does the only thing she can think to do. She kneels down on the soft sand beside Uata, frantically picking up all the contents, returning them to that claimed sacred box.

Suddenly, Shannon sees the photograph! And now suddenly, she realizes it's her time to act.

It is her moment! As a firefighter springs into action without a second thought, Shannon leaps upon Breeze. Within seconds, they reach full stride—-heading for the mountain trail.

Hola stands there for a second or two, looking at the contents of the box, strewn across the sand. Several old decks of playing cards, an old tattered zip-lock bag—-with photographs, and an old camera.

Hola grabs Malu by the arm, "I hope Shannon is not trying to be a hero—-like I wanted to be when I came to this island. We need to get the others, and go after Shannon. She may be in a heap of danger."

But Hola and Malu don't need to get the others. After the quake, Lorvin comments to some of the others, "It's a good thing we finished teaching when we did. With these earthquakes, that plateau would not be the place I would want to be."

But as soon as he says that, he sees Shannon leap upon her horse, and take to the mountain trail.

Lorvin calls out frantically to Shannon, but only his own echo returns.

Then the men—-starting with Lorvin, Christian, Sweeney, and Murray—-begin to chase after Shannon, on foot. Malu, Hola, and Feleti run quickly behind, soon passing them up. They understand their common purpose. They will in no way be able to catch the horse, but if Shannon does get injured, they will at least be able to arrive as eventual help.

The rest of the islanders join the pursuit as well—-creating a scene that looks much like a marathon event—-up the mountain trail.

Only the four women remain on the beach. They quickly find their common purpose. They kneel together on the sand—-and pray. Prayer can serve as immediate help. They don't understand the purpose of why Shannon took off so quickly, but they pray that God will protect her.

Hola has a hunch, but no one knows for sure why Shannon took off so spontaneously, and so irrationally.

Her horse doesn't understand either, but nevertheless Breeze responds to her urgency. Breeze only understands that Shannon wants him to go quickly—-and that is enough for Breeze.

Never before has Breeze gone more swiftly. Breeze doesn't even seem to be affected by the uphill climb. It is almost as if he were running on a race track.

Breeze reaches the bridge to the plateau just as the earth shakes again. Shannon sees that the bridge has shaken to the edge—a couple inches more, and it will fall deep into the canyon. But Breeze is ridden with purpose, not fear of danger.

Without hesitation, they ride swiftly over the bridge to the plateau. Shannon dismounts Breeze at the far end of the plateau. She cries out her own prayer. She doesn't know what to do at this point. But she knows she needs God's guidance.

Suddenly, Shannon hears a noise behind her. At first it startles her, but as she turns, she realizes it's Breeze.

Breeze is rearing up on his hind legs, beating his hoofs to the hard rock. Shannon expects that maybe there is a snake or other animal, hopefully not a Komodo dragon.

Shannon offers a calming hand. Breeze stops rearing and settles down. She doesn't see any snake—-or any reason why Breeze was acting that way. Maybe he could feel another earth tremor. Maybe it's best they both get out of here before the bridge slides into the canyon.

Breeze gently puts his nose forward. Then she sees it! There it is!

At the end of Breeze's extended nose, at Shannon's eye level, is a small tunnel. The space appears just big enough for Shannon to crawl through on her hands and knees. And she can see light at the end of the tunnel.

She doesn't know what is on the other end of the tunnel. Maybe this tunnel hadn't even existed before. Maybe it had been created by the last succession of earthquakes. Passing through this tunnel may reveal an entirely different world ...one filled with Komodos.

That reminds her. She reaches inside her saddle bag, and pulls out Cody Komodo. She had put that miniature stuffed animal there for a purpose. And that purpose was more than just a cute little companion or a keepsake collectible. It was a reminder to think of Leah, and to pray for her. But now, Cody has a higher calling.

She places Cody at the base of the tunnel. Her hope is that the others are following, and that they'll find her horse, and then find Cody marking the passageway, in case she is entering danger. But partly she hopes they are not following her. It's too dangerous on this mountain with all these earth tremors.

Shannon lifts herself up to the passageway, and begins crawling on hands and knees. It isn't that far. She has gone this far, she has to go on—-fear cannot have its victory. If her suspicions are correct, she has to take this chance.

Shannon's tunnel vision becomes a kaleidoscope of light as the bright rays of sunlight splash against the smooth rock face upon reaching the end of the tunnel. As she regains focus, her eyes cast upon what she had hoped to find. Yet, she is not prepared to see it.

She gasps! And for a moment, she is as motionless as that which is now before her.

Her suspicions now were that the islanders' superstitions were not wholly superstitions. She had so focused on the Holy truth of God that she'd wholly missed any truth in what the islanders were saying. She had discounted their insistence upon there being a mountain 'being', the claimed *'Man in the mountain'.*

But here he is—-and appearing to be in the same condition that the Old Chief had been in—-near death.

Shannon hurries to his side—-scraggly old hair and matted beard, motionless on his stomach with his head to the side—-but still with a pulse, as she checks the carotid artery at his neck.

Too heavy to carry, and too unmanageable to get through that small passageway ...she cries. She must desperately find a way.

It only takes a couple seconds before Shannon puts the next thought into action. She rolls him on his right side, then stretches out beside him on the ground with her back pressed against his chest. She lifts his left arm over her shoulder, then pulls it close to her. With all her effort, she then rolls onto her stomach, rolling him with her—-onto her back.

Shannon crawls on her belly with him on her back. Most of his weight is on the back of her legs, acting as a stretcher as she inches herself slowly forward on her elbows. It is not an easy task, but one she's more committed to than most anything she has ever done before. Through much gasping and eating of dirt, she manages to crawl through the passageway with the precious life cargo, in spite of the dead weight resistance.

As she reaches the end of the tunnel, she is happy to see Breeze still standing there. Shannon crawls from beneath the dead weight, quickly checks the pulse again, then lowers herself out of the tunnel opening.

She gives Breeze a big hug, then quickly moves him closer to the slight overhang of the rock. She steps up in one of the stirrups and reaches across Breeze to grab the hand with the—-*ring* on it.

A *ring*—-representing a circle of continuing love, eternal commitment, of hope—-a hope that can potentially manifest itself in a myriad of ways. This hope drives a surge of energy through Shannon's veins, providing the power to do what she must do.

But nothing is impossible with God. Shannon pulls him out over the edge and across Breeze's back. He has an old leather belt, hopefully still strong, which she hooks over the saddle horn to secure him. Her many thoughts must now focus on one, so that the mounting problems can be surmounted. They have to get out of here!

Breeze seems to know his mission. Without need of Shannon's direction, Breeze lengthens his magnificent strides towards the other end of the plateau. For all the reasons why Shannon favors an Arabian stallion, this one moment alone defines it. This is the most awesome horse she has ever seen—-or ever read about.

Breeze's powerful hoofs pound the rocky plateau, commanding submission under foot. As they near the bridge, the earth submits to another tremendous quake, a relentless bid for destruction.

Breeze falters slightly as force challenges force, powerful hoofs striking timbers that vibrate those couple inches that will no longer serve as definition of 'bridge'. But God's design for this magnificent creature provides the powerful shift from hind legs to front—-and as his front hoofs strike the solid ground on the other side, the bridge is no longer, timbers plunging into the deep canyon.

Breeze barely touches solid ground when it proves no longer such. His muscular frame strains every fiber to power into a second tremendous leap, having barely completed the first. The cliff edge and tree become part of the divided earth, falling into the canyon ...but Breeze defies all, somehow miraculously soaring toward the new cliff's edge, landing safely once again. Safety or not, he does not relent—-each stride bringing them further from the danger zone and down the mountain.

When Mom was young, she told of her dream of flying—-not on a plane or any man-made apparatus—-but actually flying. As a Christian girl, her dreams formed mostly through a Biblical perspective. Mom dreamt of angels, of whether they had wings, and how they could travel from place to place. She dreamt of chariots of fire ....and she dreamt of just being taken up into the air. As she got older, she admitted to giving up the dream of actually flying. She accepted what God had created her to be—-and tried to be quite happy and content with who she was.

Shannon, on the other hand, dreamt of horses. Her lifetime of fascination with horses never departed from her. Early on, she'd gallop around the house on all fours, playing horse. Those dreams carried into movies of White Mane, the Black Stallion, National Velvet, and Black Beauty. To ride a horse like that, it almost seemed like you were flying.

Shannon collected those pictures and others, taping them to her bedroom wall ...wall-to-wall horse pictures. There were some really beautiful horses, but never did any come close to this one.

She could not even dream this spectacular ...this is the closest she can imagine to flying.

A good three-quarter mile down the mountain, Breeze slows a bit. Tevita comes into view—-followed soon by Malu, Feleti, then Hola, and the others. They all begin jumping up and down in celebration. As they continue down the mountain trail, Lorvin, Christian, Murray, and Sweeney come into view—-not accustomed to mountain running. They approach the celebration surrounding the horse. Shannon can be seen above the dancing, upon her horse.

Lorvin catches his breath, "Thank God, you're safe! Now tell me what this is all about."

Suddenly, a lifeless body is seen stretched across the saddle. Shannon is not prepared to explain, quite yet. In part, it explains itself....the *'Man in the mountain'* is real. Tears streak her face. They do not understand the fullest extent of all this.

When they emerge from the bush, reaching the beach area, the women rush forward—-Aleah, Moriah, Onithe, and Astuti. They all rejoice, their prayers having been answered.

Aleah is the first to take notice of the condition of the man stretched out across the saddle. She has a couple of the men help lower him gently off the horse and to the ground. And she confirms that she thinks this man has the same thing as Old Chief—-what they call the serious version of missionary dysentery.

Shannon kneels down beside him. She gasps! Lowering her head to his chest, she drenches him in her tears. The *'Man in the mountain'*, now the *'Man on the beach'*, is—-but, how can it be?

"Oh, thank you, God!" Her silent prayer continues, "Please let him live! I don't believe you'd let me find him, except you'd have him live!"

Shannon tries to communicate, yet it is difficult through her sobs and tears. Malu understands hurt and anguish, and the private moments of it. He asks the islanders to provide some space here ...for their hero.

Lorvin, Moriah, Onithe, and Astuti take Shannon to the side to give their support, also eager for her explanation. Aleah doesn't leave the man's side—-the nurse in her doesn't allow her departure. She can hear what Shannon has to share later.

Shannon brings an intense amount of emotion to the side conversation. Lorvin suddenly has his own concerns. He doesn't need a translator, yet he doesn't quite know how to express it. He is quite certain he heard Shannon correctly—-he just fears what he'd heard. It possibly means that Shannon is coming down with it too ...the delirium very possibly setting in.

Lorvin agrees this should be dealt with privately. He returns to Aleah's side, his intense expression now showing his desperation, "I think Shannon might be coming down with it too. We need to get back to the Mission hospital as soon as possible. But I think it wise not to tell the islanders. They should focus on what they've learned about Jesus, and think how they are going to tell the women's island. Let's keep to our affairs and let them keep to theirs."

Aleah looks with desperate eyes, "With a statement like that, you'd soon convince me that you're coming down with it too. Openness is what we've encouraged, and they've come a long way in confessing great things. You can't mean to close them out now. We can't deny them the opportunity to pray with us."

Lorvin sees the truth in what his wife is saying, "Okay, I'll ask them to join me in prayer, but let's hurry. Have Murray and Sweeney help you with the mountain man—-and have Onithe and Astuti help escort Shannon to the ship. I'll tell the islanders goodbye for everyone."

Shannon is back beside the mountain man's side. Breeze stays faithfully beside her.

Uata rushes forward. He has the sacred box with him. Shannon looks up. Uata extends a hand, offering the box to her. She hesitates to take the box. Shannon looks into Uata's eyes. His eyes appear different. He smiles—-his grin filled with old rotting teeth, yet he smiles. His eyes are soft and gentle eyes.

Shannon takes the box. Uata nods and smiles. She slowly lifts the lid of the box, as Malu interprets, "Uata say he still believe in sacred box, but box itself not sacred, it what inside box that make box sacred."

As Shannon opens the lid, she finds the contents of the box to be missing, except for one item. Uata smiles, showing even more of those rotting teeth, as he speaks. Malu translates, "Uata say you not be new Chief ...he say, *Jesus* is chief among us."

Shannon lifts the Bible out of the box. Malu adds, "Uata ask that you tell Old Chief and *'Man in the mountain'* about Jesus too."

Shannon reaches back and grabs the reins of her horse, moved by her own feelings of passion. She hands the reins to Uata, "Here, you were keeper of the box. Now you be keeper of the horse."

Malu translates, and Uata accepts. Shannon grins, seeing Uata's eyes dance with appreciation. Uata hands Shannon a zip-lock bag. It's the old contents of the sacred box.

Feleti, Hola, and Malu agree to stay on the men's island to travel to the women's island with the new Christians. Feleti agrees to let Hola teach the women, with Malu's assistance.

Lorvin asks all of them for prayer as he departs. The last of the group to leave the island, Lorvin gives last minute instructions. Then he quickly joins the others, preparing to sail to the Mission island.

****

Once all secure on board, Lorvin again voices his concern about Shannon to his wife. Lorvin is concerned that her delirium may be intensifying. She remains at the mountain man's side, sobbing and babbling, "M-o-m, M-o-m—-I found him!"

Tears gather in Lorvin's eyes. He has been of little comfort to Shannon. She is coming down with this missionary dysentery. And she is now slipping into delirium, crying out like a child for her 'Mommy'. She had done a brave and spectacular thing, possibly saving a life. Whatever other reality she is struggling with in her mind is not so important as is their priority to make sure she gets well.

Murray and Sweeney also begin to cry as they approach. Their grandpa, Scully, had taught their dad not to cry. And in turn, Murray and Sweeney never experienced tears—-but they are crying now.

Though they had missed the missionary teaching, Murray and Sweeney had somehow caught enough here and there to gain some knowledge. Sweeney asks, "What really is sin? I know of certain things called sin—-and I have plenty of that—-but I'm bothered by a lot of other stuff too."

Lorvin realizes something at this moment. They were so busy focusing on the islanders' need to know Jesus, they had missed the very ones right here among them. Lorvin sees his wife consoling Shannon. She is doing such a good job. Maybe Lorvin can help someone too.

Lorvin wonders why it somehow seems more difficult when there is no language barrier. He doesn't know where to begin, "That's called guilt. We're all guilty of something. But guilt isn't supposed to be such a bad thing. It's supposed to point you in the right direction, not bog you down with misery. If you feel miserable though, that's okay too. It probably means you didn't take the right direction. It's like this boat—-we're desperate to get to the Mission hospital, but if we ended up going in the wrong direction we'd be miserable."

Moriah stands by her dad's side with her arm around him, also extending her heart's leading, "Sin is separation from God. And God expects us to love our neighbors as ourselves. Can we do this and still be separated from God? We can treat our neighbors better than anyone else in the world—-being the greatest company, but misery loves company. At least that's what some say. I say the first of two commandments which Jesus gave us is of foremost importance. We must love God with all our heart, soul, and mind. That means we must not only attempt to do what He says—-but also *desire* to follow His ways."

Lorvin recognizes that look on Moriah's face. And he looks at Murray and Sweeney. His daughter is having more success in getting through to them. He will not add anything. He will just listen.

Moriah continues, "When you were younger, do you ever recall your Dad asking you to do something and you simply did not do it? Or you were asked not to do something—-and you did it anyway? You may have even thought what you did wasn't wrong at all—-but it was wrong, simply because you were asked not to do it. Maybe you didn't understand why, but that doesn't matter. Your parents may have seen something that you didn't see. Maybe they wanted to protect you—-even if they had a strange way of showing they cared."

Moriah's explanation intensifies itself, "Sometimes things seem to be dictated in an unforgiving fashion and it just doesn't seem right ...or we may feel it is even very wrong. But if we disobey, does it then seem to make things right?"

Sweeney asks, "What if it wasn't our parents who mostly raised us ...what if it was a grandparent?

Moriah hesitates, "Well, I guess it's difficult to give advice when circumstances create a different context. But, ...though there are circumstances where I guess you'd be in the right not to obey, generally, whoever is your caregiver should have your best interests at heart. And you should do your best to respect them."

Murray speaks up this time, "But can't any action, whether it is deemed right or not, potentially cause someone a lifetime of pain?"

A tear travels down Sweeney's worn face, "And a lifetime of unnecessary guilt."

Moriah's call is for simplicity, "Don't carry the guilt. All anyone has to do is come clean ...confess it."

Sweeney then turns, stepping towards Shannon while breaking down in tears, "I am so sorry, Shannon."

Lorvin is confused. Is he witnessing the beauty of someone recognizing their sinful nature—-about to confess and show the desire to follow God—-or is it just shared delirium?

Shannon does not hear him, but Lorvin wonders what Sweeney is saying sorry about ...is it that he is sorry she gave up her beautiful horse?"

Sweeney will not be denied his freeing moment. He turns back towards Moriah and confesses, "Scully, I mean, Grandpa, saw that his Estie was in trouble. Estie was the name of his boat. His uncle, Mac, had given him that boat. He really loved her ...but she was on fire. Dad had just got a new motor boat, but Grandpa didn't know how reliable she was, so he took his 'old reliable'. I wanted to help, so I jumps in dad's new motor boat. Murray here, reminds me that dad had clearly said we could not use his new boat. I told Murray that when people are in danger, there is no such word as can't. Again Murray reminds me that as far as dad is concerned, bravery is no excuse for disobedience."

Lorvin adds, "Well, I think Sweeney is right ...that when people are in danger, it is sometimes okay to bend the rules. But, you can always explain afterwards why you did ...and I'm sure your parents, or grandparents, would understand."

Murray also remembers that day clearly, "I told Sweeney that I would go with him—-if he promised not to tell."

Lorvin explains, "I don't think those kind of promises or agreements should be made."

Sweeney is excited, and intensifies his speech as he tells the story, "By the time we reached the Estie, it was all fire and smoke. And Grandpa was climbing on board to save his shipmate, Doyle."

Sweeney gets into it, as if he's experiencing it at this precise moment, "You must understand ...we are real scared. At first we don't see Grandpa. He disappears into the smoke and flame. We are about to go after him ourselves, when we see him emerge out of the smoke, dragging Doyle to safety. We don't want him to see us, so we motor to the other side of Estie, and get ready to speed back before we get caught—-but then we see these two in the water, about to drown. So we save them in our boat, and take them back to where we're loading the craft ...the aircraft."

Murray recalls, "We were loading the craft with supplies for the mission field—-for somewhere out here, in Indonesia. We didn't know if the one guy we saved was going to make it. He looked in bad shape, but we knew we'd be in bad shape too. We had the other guy promise not to tell what we did ...then we go to help Grandpa pull into the dock, and see how Doyle is. The two men just sort of disappeared ...and that's about the extent of it."

Sweeney admits, "That was the extent of it ...until Rebekkah started asking questions. But Murray and I didn't want to begin stirring things up. We didn't realize one of the ones we saved was Shannon's dad ...and we had made another of those problematic promises. Honestly, we had no idea where they had gone after that ...and we figured we would just leave well enough alone. But, I know now, ...that was not well at all. And I hope you forgive me for what I've done ...I realize now that I was way wrong. You all had the right to know ...and I know what I did is unforgivable. I've had a difficult time through the years keeping that secret. And though I don't expect any forgiveness ...I am very sorry."

This is too wild! This is a sincere confession if Lorvin has ever heard one. But what are Murray and Sweeney saying? Half of it makes some sense. But, if he is hearing them correctly ...how?

****

Lorvin spends the next couple hours attempting to calm Shannon down. Spending time with Shannon, he begins to believe that she doesn't have the missionary dysentery—-and it is not delirium, but rather years of grief stored up, only to be released at this moment.

Lorvin doesn't want Shannon to set herself up like this. That they would have stowed away on that missionary plane was only conjecture. And that they would've arrived here is much wishful thinking. Maybe not on their 'wish list' back then, but renewed hope for today. Nearly two decades ago is a long time ago, and this is an unlikely scenario. It's the type of story you'd want to believe, but not likely could.

Lorvin has seen this before. Some people were not fit for the mission field. He had seen many sincere well-meaning men and women fall into an emotional breakdown. Shannon had hastily decided to come to the mission field that first time. You could tell she wasn't ready. After her year was up, she had eagerly returned home, only to quickly return to the mission field.

Aleah also shakes her head. It doesn't even look like him. This is not her brother! Aleah knows what Lorvin is thinking. Shannon must be having an emotional breakdown, desperately pretending what she wants to believe—-what she feels will save her sanity.

But, the most difficult to believe is how that story that Murray and Sweeney had told ...how could that possibly connect with what

Shannon is saying? Yet, it does connect in a way. It doesn't seem possible ...no, it's too crazy!!

Shannon takes the zip-lock bag out of her pocket, the one Uata had given her from the box. She takes out a photograph and shows it to Aleah. It is definitely—-Stephen!

Aleah begins to cry profusely.

Shannon had not only recognized the photograph to be her Dad—-she remembers that same shirt he'd worn to work on the day he'd disappeared—-the shirt that she had given him which everyone considered so ugly. And the second she had seen the photograph fall out of the claimed sacred box, she had connected the idea of the *'Man in the mountain'*. That's when she had leaped on Breeze, and breezed up the mountain.

Lorvin can still not accept all this. He needs every thread of proof. He takes the ring off the mountain man's finger and inspects it. There is an inscription on the inside of the ring—-slightly worn, but still legible. There is no date and no initials. It merely reads: *'Eternal Friends'*.

Lorvin aims to check with Cindy about the inscription. But this still seems so wild! He can't drag Cindy into an emotional breakdown too.

Shannon suddenly penetrates her tears with a burst of joy, "The birthmarks!"

Shannon puts her right arm alongside the motionless body she believes to be her Dad. His arm is sun beaten and weathered, but the birthmarks are still visible. Yes, those beautiful birthmarks.

She bursts with joy, "See! They align perfectly with mine!"

Moriah joins the joyous revelation, "Yes, I remember that. It was your birthday, and you felt bad because of some remark Stan had made about your birthmarks."

Even Lorvin begins to believe at this point—-finding it hard to believe three people would have the same exact alignment of birthmarks like this. Even as scientific and pragmatic as he is, he too is a man of faith. God had created that arrangement solely for Shannon and Dad alone ...and for this moment.

Epilogue:

Stories always go on ...whether the author writes them, they get entertained in our minds, or a new chapter of our life begins.

When one story somehow seems to end, another usually begins. Everyone's life is unique, and we all have different stories. All the chapters in our lives are not easy, but after our chapter in this life ...we have a promise from God, if we choose to accept it. My hope is that we could all share in those moments ...with Him. The purpose of this story is to help direct us to His truth. I will be concluding this story with the 5th book of this series, *'We Should Know ...'* beginning with chapter 33.

The Evolution of Confusion series:

1) So Loved ...

2) The Curious Whether and How

3) Do the Birds in the Wilderness, Not Heard, Stop Singing Their Songs?

4) The Evolution of Confusion 1 of 5 (The Essence ...)

5) The Evolution of Confusion 2 of 5 (Inevitable Outcome?)

6) The Evolution of Confusion 3 of 5 (Train Up a Child ...)

7) The Evolution of Confusion 4 or 5 (Where From Here?)

8) The Evolution of Confusion 5 of 5 (We Should Know ...)

(There are two short books outside this series, *'Chain-Link Fences'* ...with 14 short stories, & *'We Should Also Love One Another'*.)

Okay, now add *'Who Would Not Want an Inheritance?'* ...and to make an even dozen, the latest is *'What is His Name?'*

Now, a baker's dozen with *'Am I Trying to Take Away From Jesus?'.*

And now I need a break, and maybe you do too.

But, not yet ...you should finish this story first by reading the fifth part of this series, concluding with *'We Should Know'.*